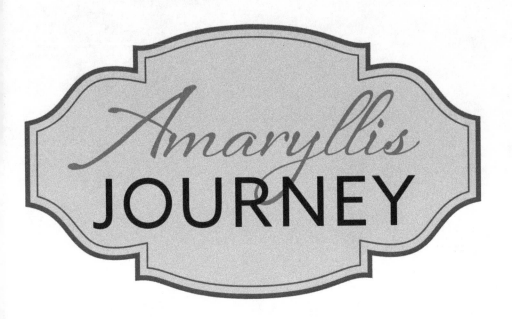

Amaryllis
JOURNEY

KONNIE K. VINER

Published by Redemption Press, PO Box 427, Enumclaw, WA 98022.

Toll-Free (844) 2REDEEM (273-3336)

Redemption Press is honored to present this title in partnership with the author. The views expressed or implied in this work are those of the author. Redemption Press provides our imprint seal representing design excellence, creative content, and high-quality production.

This is a work of fiction. Names, characters, places, and incidents either are the products of the author's imagination or are used fictitiously. Any resemblance to actual persons, living or dead, businesses, companies, events, or locales is entirely coincidental.

Unless otherwise indicated, all Scripture quotations are taken from the Good News Translation® (GNT) in Today's English Version- Second Edition Copyright © 1992 by American Bible Society. Used by permission.

ISBN: 978-1-64645-180-7 (Paperback)
978-1-64645-181-4 (ePub)
978-1-64645-182-1 (Mobi)

Library of Congress Catalog Card Number: 2020909434

Dedicated to the memory of Betty Louella,
my godly mother and mentor.

Charm can be deceiving,
and beauty fades away,
but a woman who honors the LORD
deserves to be praised.
PROVERBS 31:30 CEV

Chapter One

All that remained of her nine-year marriage was crammed into her green Toyota Corolla like a hand-packed ice cream cone. Through the thrashing rain and cascading tears, she tried to steady her focus on the road, unable to expel her ex-husband's last words from her mind. They were magnetic, playing over and over. *You're worthless, Shannon. This marriage is worthless. I deserve to be happy. We're done!*

A gray pickup sped by, throwing a pond of water and road debris onto her windshield. The wipers, already at maximum speed, couldn't squeeze off the slimy particles fast enough. Piercing the painful silence, she cried out, "I hate my life! I'll never make it on my own!"

Without conscious thought, she reached up and turned off the windshield wipers. Losing sight of the edge of the road, she spiraled through the breakdown lane.

"Pull the blanket away from her neck a bit, please. Let her breathe." Slowly the room came into focus, enough that she could see a smiling doctor and a busy nurse. The doctor moved closer. "Well, good afternoon, Miss Shannon. We're glad to have you back."

"Where . . . where am I?"

"You're in Scranton, Pennsylvania. You were involved in a motor vehicle accident last night. I'm Doctor McLachlan. Can you tell me the last thing you remember?"

She pushed words through her cotton mouth. "It . . . was pouring rain."

"Shannon, apparently you lost control of your car last night in the rain and fog. The driver of an 18-wheeler saw you go flying off the side of the road and into some trees. He called 911 and then ran to help you. EMS and local firefighters had to extricate you from the car, then they transported you here by ambulance. You have two fractured ribs, some head lacerations, and a concussion."

She raised her hand to her aching head, flinching as she touched the bandage. The doctor nodded at her reaction.

"Yes, we'll be keeping you until tomorrow to monitor your concussion. Your parents are waiting in the lobby; it's a good thing you had emergency contact numbers in your phone. Karen is here to help, so let her know if you need anything. You'll get a meal soon and something to help you relax this evening. I'm happy to see you're responding well. I'll check in on you again tomorrow. I'll let your parents know they can see you now."

"Thank you, doctor." Shannon brushed her fingers across her face, feeling for injury. There were bandages in her hairline, but her face seemed untouched. She sighed, relieved that things weren't worse. Placing her hands on the bed, she attempted to reposition, but gasped from the sharp pain in her ribs. Slowly, she maneuvered herself into a more comfortable reclining position.

The late afternoon sun kissed the walls and polished the furniture with a golden glow as nurse Karen pulled back the drapes and opened the blinds slightly. Shannon hadn't realized how dark her room had been until that moment. Karen moved the tray closer, filled Shannon's water bottle, and adjusted her bed. Shannon thanked her.

"You're a lucky lady," Karen said, then excused herself as Shannon's parents entered the room.

"Oh, Shannon! Thank the Lord, you're okay. You're a fighter, and we've been praying." Her mother's gentle hug and kiss were good medicine. "I hope I didn't jostle your ribs."

"Hey, sweetie," Shannon's dad took his turn with the hugs. "We were talking to the truck driver last night who saw what happened. I'm glad he was there to call 911 so quickly. It was foggy and already getting dark—you could've been out there all night if he hadn't been there."

An icy reality surged through Shannon's mind as she recalled turning off the wipers. *In that moment, I wanted to die.* It was a sobering realization, but now she was thankful that she was alive.

Dad gave her a quick pat, then added, "Oh, and I called your new boss. I found the number in your phone. I hope you don't mind. He said not to worry and wished you a speedy recovery. Sounds like the kind of boss you want to have."

Karen popped back in and asked if Shannon needed anything else. "No, but I would like someone to fill in the past hours, but I guess the doctor won't have much time to do that, will he?"

Karen smiled as she excused herself to tend to other patients.

Dad filled in a few brief details which the truck driver had reported, but Shannon couldn't remember anything after turning off the wipers.

Several hours of Shannon's life were missing, and that was a mind-boggling thought. But they were also hours without emotional pain, shame, or anger—and she was alive. *That's a fair trade-off*, she rationalized. *Emotional pain is the worst.*

"I'm going to head back home, honey, since there won't be room for me. Dad will transfer things from your car to a rental and take you the rest of the way to your new place."

"Okay . . ." Shannon still felt a little dazed, and wasn't sure how to react to that. Then the full impact of the words hit her.

"Oh! My car. Is it bad? Did everything get ruined?"

"Well." Dad's face was grave. "I called the garage, and your car is totaled. I took care of the claim with your insurance company. We should be able to fit everything that's not broken into my rental. It's larger than the Corolla, anyway."

"Oh my gosh. What am I gonna do?" Shannon couldn't help the moan that left her lips. Like her life hadn't been in enough of a mess before today.

"I know this sounds bad, honey." He gently squeezed her arm. "But let's focus on the fact that you're okay. It could have been so much worse."

If you only knew! Shannon shuddered as she remembered that brief moment in the rain.

"I can stay as long as you need me to help get your apartment set up. You won't be doing much until those ribs heal. And we'll get you a rental car when we get to Loughton Valley till the insurance settlement comes through."

"Okay." She yawned, the deep breath making her flinch again. "I'm still feeling a little loopy. Hopefully, it's just the pain meds. I'll try to stay awake in the car, Dad." She smiled, trying to reassure her parents.

After dinner, Shannon said goodbye to her mom and watched the news with her dad for thirty minutes before he returned to his hotel room. Once she was alone, she turned off the TV and tried to get comfortable in the bed. It was hard to concentrate, but as she dozed off, questions filled her mind with worry. *Is starting late going to impact my job? How much was damaged in the accident? What kind of car should I get? I hope the insurance is going to cover this. Oh, gosh! What about my medical bills? I should have just stayed home!*

❦

The next morning, Shannon awoke to find her dad resting in the recliner by her bed. When Dr. McLachlan came in, he reviewed the scan, procedures, surgery, and medications, and then approved her discharge. "When the wheelchair arrives, you're all set to go, Shannon. You should follow up with a doctor to monitor the effects of your concussion when you get to your new location. It was nice to meet both of you. Have a safe trip, now." With that, he shook her hand, her dad's hand, and left the room.

The nurse helped her get dressed and gather her things, then an orderly wheeled her down to the exit and waited with her while Dad pulled the rental car around. Within minutes, Shannon was settling into the car. Gingerly, she adjusted the pillows and the blanket her mom had left for her. *Sunglasses.* She didn't know where her sunglasses were . . . probably still in the Toyota.

As they pulled into the mechanic's lot, she spotted her car. She gasped aloud. "How could I not remember *that* happening?"

Dad nodded. "Your guardian angels got squished in that one, didn't they? We are so thankful you don't have serious injuries."

"Would you take a photo?"

"Already did, for the insurance company. That's a good reminder to be thankful, isn't it?"

You have no idea, Dad.

He parked next to her car, and Shannon watched as he started transferring boxes. He was right—everything fit in the rental with room to spare. Several boxes rattled when they shouldn't have, but they'd have to explore that later. Before long, they were back on the road to her new apartment.

Despite her efforts, Shannon dozed off for what she thought were a few minutes. She awoke to see a sign announcing, LOUGH-TON VALLEY, CONNECTICUT, 20 MILES.

Twenty miles to a new life. What kind of life she wasn't sure, and now she feared the worst. This accident was a bad start. She sighed. *What kind of future do I have?* Inside the city limits, another sign: LOUGHTON VALLEY, INCORPORATED 1654.

"Look, Dad. Geez, that's ancient!"

The GPS announced their destination. The Oak Crossing apartment complex was one mile ahead. It was 6:00 p.m. Traffic seemed heavy for such a little town, but people were arriving home from work. Shannon spotted the apartment directory sign in the parking lot and located the building for apartment 305. She'd chosen the third floor because it seemed safer and the stairs would be good exercise. With her painful ribs and headache, she was now regretting that decision. They checked in with the building manager, got the key, and found a parking spot close to the entrance.

At least there are trees and flowers around the building. I miss my flower gardens. I took so much for granted. Fresh flowers almost every day? That's a luxury I won't have now.

Dad was already pulling boxes from the back seat by the time Shannon eased her way into the open. She was surprised when a couple approached.

"Hi, my name's Jennifer," the blonde announced. "This is my husband, Kevin. We're in building two, next door. Can we give you a hand with unloading? We moved in a few months ago, and our backs have finally recovered." She chuckled.

Shannon smiled back. They certainly gave a good first impression of the neighborhood. Jennifer was probably in her early thirties. A bit older, Kevin appeared attentive to Jennifer. *Looks like she married the right guy . . . but who knows what really goes on in a relationship. First impressions can be deceiving.* She shook her head, determined not to get lost in negativity.

"That would be awesome. Thank you, Jennifer. I'm Shannon Enright, and this is my father, Riley Sweeney."

"Pleased to meet you both," Kevin replied. "Show us where to begin."

"Very nice to meet you also." Shannon's dad opened the trunk. Kevin helped place suitcases and boxes on the sidewalk and offered to carry the heavier items. Jennifer picked up one suitcase and a lightweight box. Shannon's dad hoisted two larger boxes and instructed Shannon to carry only her purse.

"Shannon was in a car accident and is still recovering. It's a blessing that she has such nice neighbors."

"Shannon, I'm so sorry to hear that. We'll help get you settled tonight and check in on you sometime tomorrow, if that's okay."

"That would be wonderful. Thank you for helping us move these things into the apartment."

Kevin brought the last box upstairs, then he and Jennifer said goodbye.

Shannon moved slowly through her new home. She had rented the furnished apartment online, and she was eager to see if the photos had been accurate. She wasn't disappointed; natural light permeated the space. It was clean and pleasant, decorated in neutral tones. She opened the sliding door for some fresh air, then turned slowly to sit down on the couch.

Dad looked in on her from the kitchen. He had just opened a box labeled "kitchen" and found two glasses still intact. "Your mom packed some snacks and iced tea mixes," he called. "I see there's already ice in the freezer."

Emotions took hold, and Shannon fought for control. "Dad, my life is so screwed up. I still can't even say I'm divorced. I never wanted this. Losing the house, saying goodbye to family and friends, leaving the job I loved, and now this accident? I can't imagine how things could get much worse!" Tears of pain, grief, loss, disbelief, discouragement, and sadness began to fall. "I'm so glad you're here. Things always seem better when you're around. Thanks for dropping everything and coming to help."

"That's what dads do, baby. I'll always be here for you. Nothing's going to change that, Shannon. Life is often unfair—it throws curve balls at everyone, the most unexpected, unimaginable things. You've had more than your share recently," he said, handing her a glass of sweet tea as he sat next to her. "But we know you better than anyone else. You're brave and full of life. Don't let Andrew change who you are; don't give him that power. His choices are hurtful, yes, but you had a good life before him, and you'll have a good life without him. I don't pretend to know how you're feeling, honey, but you have a good head on your shoulders. You will get through this, I promise. But he'd better not show his face around here!"

A grin lifted the corners of Shannon's mouth. She had wondered when his Irish temper would show up. He caught the look and gave her a gentle hug.

"Those two chairs on the deck look pretty inviting," he said, sipping the tea. "Why don't we go outside?"

"They do look comfy, don't they?" she responded. "The fresh air would be good for both of us."

Dad helped her to her feet, and they stepped onto the deck. Dad sat down while Shannon stood at the railing, looking out. "It really is pretty here." Light bounced from something in the distance, and she leaned forward to investigate. "Oh, look, Dad! I see a lake. Way out past those trees. Can you see it?"

"Yep. This is a beautiful place. It seems nice and peaceful too."

"Looks like there's a trail that leads to it. I'll enjoy taking that trail around the lake once my ribs are healed."

Dad nodded. "Well, you be smart about that. I'd worry about you out there alone after your head injury if you go too soon." He finished his tea and stood up. "I'm going to get back to work. What can I take into your room for you? Tell me what to put where, and I can start opening boxes and unpacking."

"Thanks, Dad." Shannon followed him back inside. "Just the blue suitcase and the box marked linens for now. We can sort everything else out tomorrow. Seems like all I've done today is sleep, but I'm getting drowsy again. Hope you don't mind if I turn in early. I'm sorry you have to sleep on the couch; I wasn't expecting company so soon."

"It's okay, don't worry about it. Things will get better. Here, I found the linens. I'll go make up the bed for you, and then I'll catch up on the news."

After a quick shower and her evening pain meds, she crawled carefully into bed, trying not to jostle her sore ribs. Thoughts were swirling, but she was determined not to dwell on them. Worries past or future—not tonight. One day at a time. Or maybe just one minute at a time.

Chapter Two

Shannon found her dad on the deck the next morning, admiring the sunrise. She smiled brightly at him, doing her best to reassure him she was feeling better.

"Good morning, Dad. You're out here early. Did you miss your bed?"

"Not too much. That's a good couch. I didn't expect you up this early either. Did I wake you?"

"No, I'm feeling pretty good today. Couldn't stay in bed any longer. We've got lots to do."

"That's true. A lot to do and a lot to be thankful for. I could go for some breakfast, but there isn't really anything here yet. I remember passing a Dunkin' on the way. Does that sound good to you?"

"Mmm . . . iced with coconut and raspberry, please. Maple donut or second choice, glazed. Thanks, Dad. Caffeine and sugar—what a great start for the day. Can't ya just hear Mom lecturing us?"

"Yep, and she's always right . . . but you know what? The cat's away. When I get back, I'll help you unpack. Then we can get a rental car for you. Don't start opening any of those boxes until I return. Doctor's orders!"

Shannon walked around the tiny apartment, slowly opening cabinet doors and drawers, organizing things in her head. *Now I know the real meaning of "downsizing."* Her furniture and possessions had once filled a lovely four-bedroom house; now everything she owned had fit in a Corolla. And a lot of that was broken. She should have fought harder for more possessions, but Andrew's parents' cutthroat attorney had quickly intimidated her into submission. What little furniture she did get hadn't been worth renting a truck to haul it. *What's done is done. Que será, será. Time to move on and start over. If I keep thinking that, maybe I'll believe it.*

The coffee and donuts were the perfect morning treat, and the day passed quickly as the two of them unpacked, organized, and re-organized. In the afternoon, they took a trip to the rental car company and did some quick grocery shopping. Finally, Dad made his famous barbecued chicken on the community grill. After dinner they strolled around the complex and located the laundry room, mail room, gym, pool and sauna, game room, and TV room. Other tenants offered friendly greetings as they passed.

Shannon was feeling the effects of the accident, but she worked hard to stay upbeat as long as Dad was around. She didn't want him to feel like he needed to stay longer than originally planned, and they'd gotten so much done that she'd have all day tomorrow to rest. Her ribs would take time to heal, she knew that, but she could finish what was left to do on her own.

At the restaurant, Shannon set her fork down in a puddle of

blueberry syrup—all that was left of her delicious breakfast. Dad pushed his plate aside at the same time and looked up.

"Well, that does it, I guess. Time to get on the road. You gonna be okay?"

Shannon nodded, keeping her smile in place. "Yep. One day at a time. Thanks for breakfast, Dad. And thanks so much for all your help. I couldn't have done this without you."

"You're welcome, sunshine. Any time." He paid the check, and the two of them headed outside. She watched as he climbed into his rental car, then leaned in for a last goodbye kiss.

"Tell Mom I love her. I'm going to be fine here. Just call me Scarlett O'Hara—after all, tomorrow is anothah day."

He laughed at her less-than-stellar Southern accent and squeezed her hand.

"Okay, but you tell us if you need anything. We aren't that far away. We'll check in with you Monday night to see how your first day at the new job went."

He put the car in gear and backed out of the parking space. Shannon leaned against her rental car and watched him go, waving and fighting back tears as he drove out of sight.

Can I do this? Or am I really the loser Andrew said I was? No. Mom and Dad taught me to be strong. I just let Andrew push me down for so long. He's not here anymore. I'm gonna be fine. But she was more afraid than she wanted to admit.

She climbed into her rental and meandered back to her empty apartment, admiring her new town along the way.

The doorbell rang through the quiet space, startling Shannon. She opened the door to find Jennifer with a bouquet of fresh daisies in a yellow-and-white teapot.

"Hope you like daisies. I know the pot is cracked, but I'll explain that later. Just checking in to see if you need anything—Kevin and I are making our Walmart run."

Shannon thought it was a bit odd to give a cracked pot as a gift, but the flowers were pretty. Maybe something happened to it on the way.

"That's so thoughtful—thank you. I think I'm all set for now. Dad and I went to the grocery store yesterday. He just left, and I'm starting my first day at work tomorrow. Do you have time to come in for some iced tea?" *Some company would be nice,* she thought. *Things are a little too lonely right now.*

"Sure. Kev's still puttering around the apartment, so he won't miss me. I won't hit you with twenty questions, but what brings you to little Loughton Valley?"

"A new job . . . and a new life. Oh! Excuse me," Shannon muttered as she grabbed another tissue. She was losing the battle with her tears.

"I'm so sorry. Are you okay? Change is hard, I know. If there's anything I can do to help, let me know. Anytime, really."

Shannon smiled weakly as her new friend rattled on.

"When you feel like talking, I'm a good listener. Had to be, growing up with four sisters. Everyone needs a four-a.m. friend—if you don't have one, feel free to call me." She wrote her phone number on the notepad on the kitchen counter and added a big smiley face. "This is a great little town. Kev and I have been here for three years, but we just moved to these apartments; they are much nicer. I'd love to show you around when you have time, maybe next weekend?"

"I'll take you up on that offer." Shannon wrote her own number and email address on another sheet of paper and handed it to Jennifer.

"It's a date. Give me a call when you're ready for a tour of the town. Of course," she chuckled, "Loughton Valley is a short tour."

Shannon found herself with a smile on her face as she closed the door behind her new neighbor. Jennifer's offer of friendship seemed genuine, and Shannon looked forward to getting to know her better.

She fixed herself a light dinner and reviewed the company brochure while she ate. Then she strolled around the complex grounds again. Despite the pleasant surroundings, her mood was far from buoyant as she locked up for the night. *I could like it here,* she thought, *but who am I kidding? I miss my family, my friends, my house, my job. I miss everything about my life.*

Lost in her thoughts and forgetting about her injuries for a moment, she reached to pull the covers back on the bed. Sharp pains from her ribs left her gasping for air, and she dropped onto the bed. Despair and frustration tumbled out in a growl.

"This is so not fair. I gave up everything. He's given up nothing . . . well, except me, and he didn't want that. And now, here I am—I can barely move! And I'm supposed to start work tomorrow. All I know is, this new job had better not be a mistake."

Fighting against tears, she gingerly pulled up the covers. Day Two was finally over.

The alarm woke her at 5:00 the next morning. She'd set it extra early for her first day on the job. She was glad she'd laid out her clothes the night before. Nerves would have had her second-guessing everything.

New Haven was only twenty minutes away, but she left with plenty of time to spare. She found parking, gathered her things, and headed into suite 214. The receptionist greeted her with a bright smile and a cheery hello.

The welcome boosted Shannon's confidence, and her smile felt natural as she introduced herself.

"Hi. I'm Shannon Enright. I'm starting here today."

"Oh, Shannon. It's so nice to see you. My name is Chloe. We were so sorry to hear about your accident." She came out from behind the desk as she spoke, genuine concern in her voice. "How are you feeling?"

"I'm doing okay," Shannon responded. "A little sore, but I'm alive and happy to be here."

"We're glad you're here too. Have a seat over there, and Jeffrey will be right out."

Jeffrey arrived moments later and led her to his spacious office, where he welcomed her, asked how she was feeling, and explained the project she would be working on initially. "Here's the investment portfolio for the company I've assigned to you. Carla, one of our senior analysts, will oversee the project and assist as needed. Her extension is listed on the inside of the folder. We have a great team, and I'm sure you'll assimilate easily. I'm always available for questions too." As he stood, he extended his hand. "Welcome aboard. Let's meet some of the crew."

Shannon followed her new boss into a large room filled with cubicles. He led her through the maze, introducing her to coworkers along the way. She was encouraged by their friendly smiles and greetings.

As they rounded the end of a row, Jeffrey motioned to an empty desk. "This is where you'll be, Shannon. Anyone here will be happy to help you bring in your personal things and help you get settled. We won't be letting you do any heavy lifting for a while."

She heard a chair roll back, and a man peered out from the next cubicle. With a smile, he stood and reached out his hand. "That's the truth—you just say the word when you need help. I'm Ryan, by the way."

"Thanks, Ryan."

Now that you've met your nearest neighbor," Jeffrey said, "I'll leave you to get settled." Shannon watched him leave, then settled in at her desk. She opened the project folder he had given her and pushed back her worry that the concussion might affect her performance. She could do this. She'd worked as a financial analyst for several years—investment portfolios, financial statements and reports, government contracts, and insurance strategies were all part of her previous responsibilities.

Her father's confident encouragement resonated again in her mind, and she felt excited to dig in and get busy. It was the best way to keep her mind occupied.

The week passed quickly, and Shannon became comfortable in her new surroundings. By Friday, she was feeling a little better about her decision to start her life over in Loughton Valley.

Chapter Three 🌹

Saturday afternoon, Jennifer called and asked if Shannon was ready for her tour of the town.

"I would love to see the town," Shannon replied, "but I might have to rest a few times along the way. I'm still pretty sore from the accident."

"No problem." Jennifer replied. "We'll take all the time you need."

It was a beautiful day for a walk around the town square, and Jennifer enthusiastically pointed out the historic buildings, businesses, and commemorative war memorials that lined the brick sidewalks. Shannon was impressed.

"I love the shops around the square. They're so quaint. Are they original to the town?"

"Well, a fire destroyed most of the original wooden structures. There are still a couple buildings here that are three hundred years old, but most of what you see was built in the late 1800s. We have two that are on the National Register of Historic Places."

Majestic, mature oaks lined the streets. A lovely gazebo, framed by magenta and yellow roses, graced the town's center square. Several stately maples provided shade for the picturesque grouping. Shannon stopped to rest on a bench near a large water fountain, admiring the flowers and other landscaping that showed a deep sense of pride in the town.

Toward the end of the square, Shannon stopped again to examine an old hitching post and horse trough. "It's so lovely and peaceful here. I could get used to this."

Jennifer nodded. "Oh, I know. I love it here. But come on— let's go down Crown Street. I've saved the best place for last."

Turning the corner, Shannon spotted a lovely little shop with an array of potted plants outside. A hand-painted sign proclaimed it to be "The Amaryllis."

"Welcome to my favorite place in town—Rose Daniels' shop. Everyone loves her." Jennifer raved. "She's part of the glue that holds this town together—her and this magical place. You'll spend hours here. I try to stop by for at least a few minutes every weekend." She pushed the door open, and the two stepped into the little shop.

A bell over the door announced their arrival, and an older lady with a huge smile and gray hair twisted into a bun emerged from the corner with flowers in one hand and a ceramic pitcher in the other. Half the handle was missing on the pitcher. "Good morning, Jennifer."

"Good morning, Rose. This is my new friend, Shannon Enright. She just moved to town last weekend, and she's living in my apartment complex—aren't I the lucky one. I'm giving her the royal tour."

"Welcome, Shannon. Look around and have a complimentary cup of coffee or tea and a pastry in our shop next door. Before you leave, please choose some flowers from the gardens out back for a fresh bouquet for your new apartment . . . no charge. It will be my housewarming gift to you." Rose smiled and turned to wait on two customers.

"Thank you, ma'am." Shannon responded. "I would appreciate that."

Rows of flowerpots and other knickknacks were interspersed with large containers of fresh flowers and foliage. The heady scent and riotous colors filled Shannon's senses. A double sliding glass door at the back of the store allowed a peek out at a beautiful garden area outside.

Shannon continued surveying the room, walking slowly past shelves that contained pitchers, vases, hat boxes, old milk bottles, bowls, cookie jars, beach pails, and even a few bird cages. Framed pictures of flowers, woodland scenes, mountains, beaches, printed sayings, and Bible verses adorned the walls and shelves.

She noticed a large crack in a lovely blue pitcher, and remembered the broken-handled one Rose had been holding. Curious, she stopped to look closer and realized that most of the items were damaged or broken. And yet, every piece had a price tag. *How weird,* she thought. *Why would anyone buy something so obviously broken?*

Shannon followed Jennifer to a large, open French door on the side wall.

"Would you like some tea, Shannon?" Jennifer asked. "This is Rose's Tea Cozy."

"That would be great. Herbal tea, please. Something fruity."

Jennifer headed straight for a self-serve counter in the corner of the room. Potted plants and floral arrangements decorated this room also. Customers were seated at tables scattered around the room. White tablecloths covered three round tables, each with a floral centerpiece, a mug full of colorful markers, and a sign announcing it was a "thankfulness table."

Looking closer, Shannon noticed handwritten notes, including names, initials, and dates, written on the plain tablecloths. *What on earth?* Colorful patchwork tablecloths covered the other two tables, also with floral centerpieces and baskets filled with index cards.

Jennifer crossed the room carrying a tray with a china teapot and matching cups and saucers. She set it down on one of the patchwork-covered tables.

"Let's sit here, Shannon." She pulled out two chairs, then filled the cups with a fragrant, steaming tea. As they got comfortable, Jennifer reached out to pick up the pile of index cards from the center of the table. "Oh, good," she said. "Looks like Rose has put out new conversation starters."

"Conversation what?" Shannon laughed, but she was intrigued. "And what are thankfulness tables?"

"Conversation starters are Rose's way of getting us to talk to each other, to learn about each other. And the thankfulness tables—when something great happens that we want to share, we write it out on the tablecloth. When one fills up, she hangs it on the wall over there for a while and puts out a new one."

Shannon shook her head. "This has to be the most unique place I've ever been. So tell me something—what's with all the chips and cracks in her merchandise?"

"Oh, you noticed." Jennifer grinned.

"They're kind of hard to miss. People buy this damaged stuff? I mean, it's pretty, but . . ."

"Well, yeah. Every piece here is damaged in some way, but Rose fixes them up and uses them for her bouquets. And all those beads and lace, shells and buttons—they cover the broken places and other flaws."

"But why?" Shannon asked. "Why does she use broken things to start with?" A soft chuckle behind her made Shannon turn. She felt her cheeks flush as she realized Rose had heard her question.

"I brought you two a little something to tide you over until dinner," the proprietor said, placing a basket of fresh blueberry scones on the table. The fragrance was heavenly. Rose pulled out the chair next to Shannon and sat down.

"Why do I use broken things? I get asked that question a lot, Shannon. The simple answer is that *broken* doesn't mean useless or worthless. The original beauty is still there; it just needs to be repaired a bit. Actually, I think most of these items are more beautiful because of the repairs." She reached out and traced a string of tiny pearls that followed a crack on the table's centerpiece.

"The containers in my shop are still useful to hold God's beautiful creations—the beauty of the flowers is never diminished by the container. We're like these pots, you know. We're all broken in one way or another. You can't go through life without some cracks and chips." The bell over the door jangled. "Oh, excuse me a minute," Rose said. "I have a new customer."

Jennifer pointed toward an antique cash register. "See that large punchbowl next to the register? It's filled with broken items that Rose's customers bring in—pieces of china, glass, pottery, key chains, jewelry, picture frames, ornaments, knickknacks, shells—anything Rose can use to repair the broken containers."

Shannon looked more carefully at the teapot filled with flowers at the center of their table. She admired the small pearls and pieces of jewelry concealing the break near the handle. She glanced at Jennifer. "I noticed even the pin she's wearing has a big crack in it."

"I know." Jennifer looked thoughtful. "I've never seen Rose without that pink amaryllis pin. She wears it with everything. Doesn't matter the color or whether she's dressed fancy or comfy, she's wearing it. She says it's her most precious possession because her late husband gave it to her. I heard he died after a hiking accident in the Rocky Mountains. I did ask her once how it got broken. She just smiled and said it didn't matter, the pin was still beautiful to her. She doesn't have any family nearby—or if she does, they never visit. I think that pin must be a connection to happier times."

"Can't imagine her seeming any more happy. She's a bundle of joy."

Rose returned to their table. "I'm sorry for the interruption. I don't think I finished answering your question, Shannon. You see, everyone has experienced brokenness, but we're still as beautiful and useful to God as we were before. In fact, often we're more beautiful to Him and others because of what we've been through in life. We're all perfectly imperfect through God's grace. Now, don't forget to visit the gardens out back. Bring your flowers to the desk before you leave." She tapped Shannon's shoulder gently, then returned to the floral-arranging counter at the front of the floral shop.

Shannon watched her leave, and for a moment, bitterness at her current situation clouded her thoughts. *What could someone so joyful and happy know about being broken, anyway?* She picked up her cup and finished the last sip of tea. Whatever, she wasn't going to let it spoil the day. She turned a bright smile her new friend's way.

"Thank you, Jennifer, for showing me around town and introducing me to Rose. She's a unique character, all right. I see why you said this is a magical place. I'll go select a few flowers, and then we should probably head back. I don't want to keep you away from Kevin for too long."

"Oh, no worries," Jennifer assured her. "I told him we would stop here, so he'll understand. He loves her too."

They wandered down a meandering path of stepping-stones, through a white, arched trellis covered with roses, and into the cutting garden. The flowers were beautiful. Wildflowers were in the front, annuals in the middle, and perennials in the back. Shannon recognized most varieties. *It's a larger version of my gardens*, she thought. Then she looked away quickly before that image could drag her back to what she'd lost. She caught sight of a charming brick cottage at the back of the property. More lovely blooms surrounded it. "Who lives there?"

"That's Rose's cottage."

"She lives there? It's beautiful; very quaint."

Rose joined them in the garden. "Do you like sunflowers, Shannon?" she asked.

"They're one of my favorite flowers. That's where I was headed."

Shannon gathered five stalks of dwarf sunflowers, then followed Rose back to the cutting counter.

"Excellent choices." Rose cut off some leaves and stem ends, then turned around and surveyed the containers behind her. "Ahh! This one is perfect—do you like it?" It was a large, cream-colored ceramic pitcher with bits of yellow pottery and light brown glass glued in the shape of a sunflower in the center.

"It's lovely, thank you."

Rose touched the brown glass gently. "This is sea glass," she explained. "Some of my customers bring in pieces they find along the beach. I love the warm glow of glass that's been polished by the waves and sand." She carefully arranged the sunflowers and some greenery in the pitcher and handed it to Shannon.

"Thank you, Rose. It's beautiful. And so gracious of you—I'll think of you every time I look at my sunflowers on the kitchen table. They will really brighten up my apartment."

"Here, let me carry the pitcher for you," Jennifer interjected. "Those ribs must still be sore."

"Thank you, Jennifer. They are better, but I sure look forward to getting back to normal."

Saying goodbye to Rose, Jennifer and Shannon retraced their steps through the town square on their way back to the complex. Along the way, Jennifer pointed out a few more landmarks and shops. It was obvious she was proud of her little town. And quite fond of Rose and her shop.

"How long have you lived here, Jen? Can I call you Jen?"

"Sure, everyone does. I was born here, actually. My parents moved to Hartford when I was little. I stayed there through college, but then Kev and I moved here when we got married. His job is a half hour north. Mine is forty-five minutes in the opposite direction, so Loughton Valley seemed like the perfect location, right in the middle. I teach fourth grade in Hamilton. I have such a scenic drive to work—all back roads, along the river. I don't mind the distance at all. So, how's your new job going?"

"The first week went well. I'm still a little nervous, but I think it got better by the end of the week. It's stressful to move to a new town and start a new job all at once."

"I hear ya. Let me know if there's anything I can do to help. I remember my first day on the job. Keep in mind that everyone has a learning curve. It helped me to view the challenges as adventures and not be so hard on myself. You'll do fine. It's an opportunity to prove what you can do, girl. You go!"

Shannon smiled at her encouragement. *I like her*, she thought. *This feels like the start of a great friendship.* They approached Shannon's building, and she thanked Jen again for the tour and for introducing her to Rose.

"I'll be in touch," Jennifer promised. "Best of luck with week two on the job."

Shannon placed her bouquet on the kitchen table, added more water, and looked more closely at the vibrant golden flowers—they really did add sunshine to the apartment. Smiling quietly, she filled a favorite mug with coffee and snuggled into the recliner, glad that she could finally find a comfortable position. She propped a pillow behind her back and covered herself with a colorful floral quilt—hand sewn long ago by Mom. It was the little things that would make this place feel like home.

She tried to focus on the book in front of her, but troubling thoughts tumbled through her mind once again. Could she really support herself? She was so upset with Andrew—no, she hated him for what he'd done. And her job—how many times had Andrew mocked her ability to do anything in business? Sure, she knew how to crunch numbers, but she hadn't lived on just her income before. She'd never planned to be alone, to have to deal with finances and all the other things that were haunting her now.

Jeffrey had mentioned several times through the week that he was pleased with her progress in a short span of time, so she made herself focus on that and eventually felt a little better about herself.

Still, the demeaning, vengeful, disrespectful things Andrew had said to her so many times insisted on playing back through her mind. *Nope*, she told herself, *it's time to replace those old memories with new ones—being successful in a new job and making new friends is a good start.*

Early Sunday, she took another walk around the complex, read the local newspaper (small as it was), and looked for a movie on TV. It was a lazy day, but she indulged herself. She planned her attire for the next week, did a load of laundry, fixed a light dinner, and got ready for bed. Hopefully, she'd have no nightmares tonight. Between her emerging memories of the accident and Andrew's rejection on constant replay, sleep had become a valuable commodity.

Arriving early at work on Monday morning, she was surprised to find a small bouquet of flowers on her desk. It wasn't hard to tell where they came from—the mason jar they were in had a repaired chip. The attached note read, "Glad you joined our department, Shannon," and it was signed by Carla, the analyst who'd been helping with her training. They'd shared lunch on Friday, and Shannon was enjoying getting to know her.

Shannon walked down the hall to her cubicle. "Carla, thank you very much. This is so thoughtful; the poppies are beautiful. Did they come from the Amaryllis? I met Rose on Saturday. She's amazing."

"You're welcome. Yes, I still remember my first bouquet from the Amaryllis, and I still use the chipped vase it came in. It's tall and green with pieces of blue-patterned china glued around the base. I love it. I always sense Rose's love as she patches her containers. And I remember what she said when I first met her in her shop—'It was fate that brought you here; you've forgotten how beautiful you are, inside and out.' I'll never forget those words. I was an emotional mess that day, and she helped me find myself again."

"I could tell she's a special lady. I'm sure I'll be visiting her shop often. Hopefully, her joyfulness is contagious—I could use a good dose."

"It's contagious for sure. She speaks the truth and sees the beauty in everyone. She's like a mother to me now. I go to her for advice all the time, and she's never steered me in the wrong direction. I miss my mom—she's been gone for four years. I know she would have loved Rose."

"It's great that you can go to Rose like that. I get the impression that everyone loves her," Shannon said. "Something about her is so intriguing."

A few minutes more of chatter, and Shannon returned to her cubicle. The rest of the day passed uneventfully. She was finding her stride and feeling like she would be a productive part of the team.

Chapter Four

The bell over the door rang, and Rose hurried in from the garden, flowers in hand. A pastor from the local church had arrived, bringing with him a young woman whose eyes were red and puffy from tears. Quietly, Rose let her assistant know she was taking a break, then shifted the flowers to one arm and moved to greet her visitors.

"Hi, Pastor Dalton." She extended her free hand.

"Good morning, Rose. This is Libby Blevins; I called you about her this morning. Thank you for letting her stay with you until we have an opening at the shelter."

"Of course." Her smile warmed the room. "Hi, Libby. I have my spare bedroom all set up for you. Thanks for bringing her, Pastor."

He nodded and turned to the young woman. "You have my card—feel free to call if you need anything. I'll let Rose know as soon as I hear from the shelter."

Libby thanked him meekly and wiped away tears as he left.

Rose placed the flowers in a holding container, then put her arm around her guest. "Libby, you'll be safe here. We'll take good care of you, I promise. Pastor Dalton gave me the name and address of your counselor, and I'll be driving you to your appointments. I believe the first one is tomorrow; is that right?"

"Yes, ma'am. Thank you so much for taking me in. I was afraid I'd be sleeping in the park again tonight." Worry and stress were written on her face and in her bloodshot eyes.

"You don't have to worry about that happening. I'm so glad Pastor Dalton brought you here."

"Me too—more than you know."

Rose's weekday assistant, Moriah, nodded from the counter. "Hi, Libby," she said brightly. "Don't worry, Rose; I've got the shop."

"Thanks, Moriah." Rose led Libby through the shop, out the back door to the cottage, and up the stairs to a back bedroom furnished with a twin bed, dresser, and chair. Fresh flowers adorned the side table next to the upholstered chair.

"Once you get settled in your room," Rose said, "please come back to the shop for something to eat. After that, you can rest or explore the gardens, relax on the benches and enjoy the flowers, or just grab a book and read here in the cottage."

Libby placed her backpack beside the table.

Rose continued, her voice soothing and reassuring. "I've contacted my friend at the consignment shop. We'll drop by after your appointment tomorrow to get you some clothing. Do you have pajamas? If not, there are some clean items in the dresser—help yourself. Oh, and there are toiletries and towels in the bathroom down the hall."

Libby looked at her, drooping with fatigue. "I'm very grateful . . . for everything."

"And you are very welcome."

"Thank you."

A hand-painted plaque decorated the wall above the chair, and

Libby moved closer to examine it. Her voice shook as she read, "'You, Lord, are all I have, and you give me all I need; my future is in your hands.' Psalm 16:5. That's beautiful. It's exactly what I need right now."

"I do hope it gives you comfort, Libby. He is all that we need. This is God's house—He owns everything. I'm just the caretaker. He provides everything for His children. I'll let you get settled and freshened up. See you back at the shop when you're ready."

Rose popped into her room briefly to make some notations about Libby in her prayer journal. Shannon came to mind too. She bowed her head. "Lord Jesus, Shannon and Libby need Your healing. I don't know the details of Shannon's life yet, but I could see her pain. You know what she needs. Libby is in crisis today. Let me help keep her safe, Lord. Touch the broken places in both their hearts and souls and let them know how much You love them. Use me as an instrument of Your love and give me wisdom to be an encourager. May they see Your hand working in their lives to restore what has been broken. And may they come to know You in a deeper way through their pain. You are faithful, Lord, always faithful. Bless these two beautiful women in ways that only You can. Amen."

On the way back to the shop, she acknowledged the ringing bell. "I'll be right there. Now, let's see. Oh, Mrs. Lee—you ordered the birthday bouquet, right?"

"Yes, and it's lovely," the customer exclaimed when she saw the pink and white bouquet in an old music box. "Aimee will love it. It's perfect. And I love your repairs, Rose. You are so creative."

"Well, thank you. I love restoring what was once damaged. I don't get many music boxes coming into the shop, so when this one came in, I knew Aimee would like it. The dainty ballerina that was inside was still intact, so I glued it on the outside for her to enjoy. Wish her a happy birthday for me." Rose smiled as she passed the bouquet over the counter and collected payment.

"Thank you, I will."

Glancing through the sliding door, Rose noticed Libby strolling through the gardens and joined her.

"It's beautiful here, so peaceful," Libby said. "I worked at a nursery for a while before I got married," Tears seeped out when she spoke the word *married*. "I know how much work it takes to keep plants this healthy."

"I could use some help, actually. Plants are on their own timetable, and just when you think you're caught up, another one needs attention. I can pay you for a few hours a day, if you're interested."

"I would love that. I tried to read a bit in the room, but my mind is too distracted, moving in a hundred directions. Working in the gardens would be great. Could I start now?"

"Wonderful. There are some clippers and gloves in the potting shed." Rose motioned to the back. "The annuals need deadheading—that's a good place to start. Keep track of your time and fill out a timesheet by the register. Dinner is at six—meet me back at the cottage if you're hungry, and we'll have some of the stew I have cooking in the Crock-Pot."

"Thank you. I would like that. See you then." Libby managed a small smile and walked enthusiastically toward the shed.

Rose watched her go, then turned back to her work counter, and began repairing another teapot. She hummed an old hymn as she worked, and soon the tune turned into a prayer, "Lord, walk with Libby and talk with her in the garden—tell her she is Your own."

The afternoon passed quickly, and Rose was surprised when Hailey, her evening volunteer, breezed through the front door.

"Oh my," Rose exclaimed. "Is it six o'clock already?"

"Sure is. Where do you need me tonight, Rose?"

Rose gave the girl some quick instruction, then hung her apron on a hook by the work counter and hurried out the door. Minutes later, she bustled into the cottage to set the kitchen table.

"It smells delicious, Rose." Appearing more rested, Libby joined her in the kitchen. "Can I help?"

"No, dear. I've got everything ready. You just have a seat." Rose set the Crock-Pot on the table. "Mmm, let's see if this stew lives up to its smell." She grinned as she scooped the stew into the bowls and added corn muffins to each plate. Then she sat down across from Libby. "Now, let's pray and thank God for bringing you here." Libby bowed her head as Rose prayed.

"The room upstairs is very welcoming," Libby said shyly. "I really appreciate you allowing me to stay here. I haven't had a home-cooked meal for a while. Thank you."

"My pleasure, dear. Now, tell me a little bit about yourself."

Libby sighed and began slowly. "Depends on whether you want to hear about my old life or my life now."

"You start wherever you wish."

Buttering a muffin, Libby spoke softly. "I got married during college, about five years ago. Everything was great for a year or two and I wanted to try to get pregnant, but Rob, my husband, got real upset whenever I mentioned it—said he wasn't ready."

She sighed more deeply. "I knew something was wrong, but I didn't know what. He wouldn't talk about it, he just pulled more into himself. Then he started drinking . . . a lot. He lost his job last year and instead of trying to get another job, he sat home and drank. When I came home from work, he was usually asleep on the couch. Then the fights started." She paused, and her gaze shifted uncomfortably. "It was just words at first. But something was different. I felt like I didn't know him anymore. I tried to get him to see a counselor, but he said he wasn't depressed and didn't want anybody knowing 'his business.' That's when I started talking to Pastor Dalton at church. I didn't want to talk to my parents or friends about it. I was so embarrassed. Everyone thought we were a happy couple. Then, six months ago, my company downsized, and I got laid off. Last month, we lost our home and moved into a one-bedroom apartment. And now—everything's just falling apart!"

"Libby, I'm so sorry." Rose gently patted her hand on the table. "You must have felt quite alone."

"Completely alone. And helpless . . . and trapped. I've been walking on eggshells all the time—the least little thing sets him off. I'm actually kind of glad we don't have children now. His anger has been getting worse and worse—" She stopped midsentence, wiping tears. "Then a week ago, he went into a rage over some silly thing and . . . and he hit me. I called 911. I was so afraid, especially of what I saw in his eyes." She dropped her head on her arms and sobbed.

"Oh, dear. You have been through a lot." Rose reached out to pat Libby's hand. "Thank you for sharing that with me. I know it's hard. We can talk about something else if you'd like."

Libby took another deep breath, trying to regain her composure. "No. I'm okay. It sort of feels good to get this out. You're the first person I've told, besides Pastor Dalton and the police."

"Well, Officer Garonna called this afternoon. He wanted you to know that your husband has been arrested, and it doesn't look like he will make bail."

"Is it horrible for me to say that I'm glad? I didn't want to press charges, but the police officer and advocate explained the restraining order process, and it seemed like the right thing to do. I've been so afraid of him lately. At first I thought it was because of the drinking, but then he got more aggressive when he wasn't drinking too. Sometimes, he just snaps. It doesn't make any sense. What did I do to make him so angry all the time?"

"No, Libby. Your actions should not cause him to become abusive toward you. Your husband is not healthy. You have to understand—this is not your fault. You do not deserve to be treated this way by *anyone*. You've made some courageous decisions in order to keep yourself safe. I commend you for that."

"Thank you. Pastor Dalton and my advocate have been wonderful too. I'm looking forward to starting with the counselor tomorrow. I know I need some help in processing all this and moving forward. I think it's time to let my parents know what's going on—they live in Idaho. They'll be devastated. They've always liked Rob and been happy for me. But Rob doesn't seem interested in making any changes—he says I'm the one who needs to change. When the police arrived, he was still yelling at me, blaming me."

"Can you tell me why you were sleeping in the park?"

"My neighbor called 911 two days ago because Rob was freaking out in the parking lot when I got home from the store. He went crazy, yelling at me for being late, saying I was having an affair. Can you imagine?! Then he started threatening me. I was so embarrassed and kept asking him to stop, but everything escalated. He shoved me hard against the car. I ran inside and locked the door. A few minutes later, the police arrived. I told them we would work things out and I was okay, so they left. But things weren't okay—I just didn't know how to respond, and I was afraid of making him more angry."

"That must have been very traumatic." Rose poured a second cup of tea for Libby.

"It was horrible. Later that evening, I was getting ready for bed, and Rob stormed into the bedroom yelling at me again because the police had come to the apartment—like it was all my fault. He wouldn't stop yelling. I was afraid. I just wanted to leave and get away from the yelling. I felt like my head was going to burst. So I threw on some clothes and a jacket and walked to the park in our neighborhood—needed fresh air, you know. I must have walked around for thirty minutes or so, then I decided to go back home. But I hadn't taken my keys or phone, and the doors were locked. I banged on the door, but Rob wouldn't let me in. The car was there, so I knew he was still inside."

She turned her head and looked out the window for a moment.

"I sat on the front steps, crying, but I didn't want to make a scene at the apartments, so after a while I went back to the park and eventually fell asleep on a bench. Early the next morning, I walked to Pastor Dalton's office. He took me to the police station. I guess you know the rest."

"We'll get you through this. You are stronger than you realize, Libby. I can tell. I've known Pastor Dalton for several years; he'll be a great help for you. Now that Rob is in jail, would you like to return to your apartment tomorrow to pick up a few things? Or, if you prefer, you can stay here awhile longer. Whatever you're most comfortable with. Of course, you can still work here if you like, at least until you find another job."

"Oh, how can I ever thank you?" Libby cried. "You've been so hospitable, and I've just poured out all this ugly stuff to you."

"You are lovely, Libby. Some ugly things have happened to you, painful things, but you are a lovely person—inside and out. I do hope you believe that."

"Sure don't feel lovely or loveable, but thank you for saying so. I'm still scared—not about physical harm, but about my future, you know? So many unknowns—that's the scariest of all."

"That's so true." Rose's dark brown eyes conveyed a knowing. "But we can only take each day as it comes and ask God for wisdom, guidance, and provision. Now, I have to go close up the shop. How does a nice long, hot bubble bath sound? There's everything you need in the bathroom. Sweet dreams, dear. I'll see you in the morning."

Chapter Five 🌹

*R*eturning from her early Saturday morning run, Shannon fixed a protein shake and sat on the deck for a few minutes, admiring the colorful fall leaves and bright sunshine. Her best friend from home, Claire, had called the night before and asked if she could come visit for the weekend. Shannon was delighted.

After a quick shower, she headed out to the store for a few groceries and some of Claire's favorite snacks, reflecting on their friendship. She really had missed her friend, the faithful one who'd helped her survive the shock when Andrew left. They had exchanged many text messages since she'd moved to Loughton Valley, but she'd missed their long talks. Now she had more pleasant things to talk about, and she was looking forward to showing off her new town.

Claire arrived at 11:45, and they exchanged hugs in the doorway. "Your apartment is adorable. I love the way you've decorated it."

"Thanks. I'm getting used to the smaller space. I've been working long hours, so I'm not really here much. It's perfect for me right now. I've met several neighbors—all very friendly. Do you want to rest a bit here or head to the restaurant?"

"Let's do lunch. You know me, I'm always hungry."

They enjoyed a meal at the Victorian Café in the village, chattering the whole time and catching up with each other. After lunch, they walked around the square.

"This is such a cute little town. It must be a big change after living in the city. Do you like it?"

"It's very different. I had my doubts at first—thought I'd be bored. But it's so peaceful here. It's a great place to forget the past and start over."

Claire gave her a sideways grin. "So . . . have you met any cute guys?"

"Ha! No. I don't have time to date anyway. I have been thinking about getting a puppy though. My neighbor just adopted a German Shepherd, and she told me there was a sibling still left at the shelter. I visited once. The cutest little female. If she's still there on Monday, I think she's coming home with me. As soon as our eyes met, I felt like she was going to be mine."

"That's exciting. A puppy would be great company for you."

Back at the apartment, they continued chatting away, just like old times.

"I'm glad you came to visit. I thought about going to see you a couple of times because I've missed you, but I'm not ready to be back in town. I hope you understand. You know, afraid of running into Andrew and his girlfriend." Shannon's mood changed. "I couldn't handle that."

Claire looked uncomfortable. "Umm, Shannon . . . I had to come see you this weekend because . . . umm . . . there's something I have to tell you."

"What? Nothing could be worse than the night Andrew announced he was leaving, barely two weeks after we moved into our new home."

"I wish that were true." Claire frowned, then took a breath. "Uh . . . Lela is pregnant."

The words hit Shannon like a bombshell. Her body absorbed the shock, rocked from the impact. Her heart stopped. She felt it. And then it started again, pounding, shaking her being, as what was left of her world imploded. All she could see was Andrew and that woman. And now, a baby.

Claire jumped up and moved over to her side. "I'm so, so sorry, Shannon. I didn't want you to hear it from anyone else. I had to tell you in person." Silence, as moments passed like eternity. "Shannon?" She tried gently to get her attention. "Talk to me."

With an effort, Shannon drew herself back to the room. She pulled her arm away from Claire's touch, shaking her head. "You know—I thought I could go on with my life and press through like everyone else does. People get divorced and move on every day, right? And really, as hard as it's been the last three months, I thought I was doing okay. But this?" She lurched to her feet and began pacing the room. "I'm here dealing with his deceit, rejection, and lies, but he gets to enjoy having a baby, being a *father?*"

Swallowing her sobs, Shannon tried to compose herself. "I went through years of infertility treatments, you know that. So, this is the 'new life' he said he wanted, instead of being married to me?" Suddenly, she froze, looking at her friend wide-eyed. "Wait—so how far along is she? And how did you find out?"

"Mark ran into them at Home Depot. It was obvious she was pregnant. Andrew said—" She paused to clear her throat. "The . . . the baby is due in January." She braced herself for the response.

"January?" Shannon calculated backward quickly. "So . . . he knew in July when he left. He fathered a child while he was married to me!" She sank back onto the couch and the dam broke. An agonized wail broke from her lips as raw emotion assailed her. She spent minutes hunched over in real, gut-wrenching pain, both emotional and physical.

Finally, she looked up at Claire. "I never told you this, but I called him at work a few days after he left. I told him I still loved him. He said, 'I know, but things can't be changed now. I'm sorry.' And he hung up. I'm such an idiot. I made a complete fool of myself. *Things can't be changed now?* He meant the baby, Claire. His baby!"

Claire wrapped her arms around Shannon as she sobbed. After a few minutes, Shannon excused herself to the bathroom. When she returned, Claire spoke quietly. "Mark and I both feel terrible about this. We want to support you anyway we can. Is there anything we can do?"

Shannon shook her head. "Mark's a great husband. You're lucky, Claire." She wandered over to the sliding door and stood there, staring outside.

Suddenly, she turned, anger distorting her features. "Why is God allowing all this? Why is He punishing me? He knows how much I wanted a baby, but He gives one to Andrew instead? Am I such a horrible person to deserve this? Am I unlovable?"

"No, you're talking crazy now. You know none of that is true. Andrew owns this, one hundred percent. He made the choices that led to this. He dishonored his vows to you and to God. He broke the covenant of your marriage. You didn't do that. And don't worry—there are consequences. He might think everything is great now, but the consequences will come, and it won't be a pretty picture then."

Shannon began pacing again. "You know, I haven't told anyone this, but my accident wasn't completely an accident. On my way here, I wanted to die, and I did something dumb—I turned off my windshield wipers in the thunderstorm and lost control of the car. My parents don't know. I could have been killed. But I couldn't deal with it anymore. I felt like a failure, and I kept hearing all the cruel things he said before he told me he was leaving. And I didn't care. I really—I just wanted to die."

She hadn't said those words aloud before, and the enormity of the truth hit her head-on. "Oh, my God," she whispered. "I really did."

Claire's eyes were huge and filled with tears as she grabbed her friend's hands and drew her close. "It's okay. You're still here. Whatever happened that night, you're still here."

"And I am glad about that," Shannon admitted. "I have a lot to be thankful for. I know how much I would have hurt my family." She stopped and was quiet for a moment.

"Ugh, I'm so embarrassed. I was so weak at that moment. I just wanted a second chance. Part of me still loved him, that's why I called him. But not now. I hate what he's done. He's destroyed my dreams, my life. I loved him so much. I couldn't really get angry before because I still loved him. But now I'm angry. I'm really angry." She stormed into the kitchen and began pulling things from the cupboard.

"I need some tea. You want some tea?"

"Sure." Claire followed her to the doorway and stood watching, ready to help. Shannon slammed the water kettle on the stove and waited for the water to heat. Claire chose two teabags from a box and readied the cups. Shannon busied herself, looking through a cabinet, picking things up and putting them back down.

When the tea was made, they returned to the living room, where Shannon settled on the couch, holding her cup in both hands, feeling the warmth, and breathing in the fruity fragrance. They sat silent for a few minutes, sipping their tea.

Suddenly, she took a breath and rose again, her cheeks flushed. "Do you know how Andrew told me he was leaving? Three stupid sentences—that's all he needed to ruin my life." She counted them off on her fingers. "One: I'm leaving. Two: I'm not happy. Three: I don't want to be married anymore. Ha! Three simple statements, right? Only I've heard them a million times since, reverberating in my mind. And every time I hear them, it hurts more. I thought that's all he could do to me. But this—"

Her voice broke, and she dropped to the edge of the couch. "Lela's pregnant? I don't even know what to say."

She raised tear-drenched eyes to her friend's somber face. "How could he, Claire? *How could he?*"

"I don't know, honey. I really don't. I'm sorry I had to be the one to tell you. I don't know what else to say."

"It's okay. You're the only one I would've wanted to tell me. You're the best friend anyone ever had."

Shannon wiped her tears with a ferocious motion and stood up. "You know what? I'm done with this. Stay here—I'll be right back." She hurried to her bedroom, then returned with a large cardboard box. She placed it on the floor next to Claire.

"My wedding album is in there and some letters and stuff. I've looked through them too many times. Sometimes I cried, sometimes I yelled, sometimes I just stared at the pictures. I couldn't bring myself to throw them away. I knew in my head there wasn't any hope, but my heart wouldn't listen. Now all hope is dead. Stone cold dead. Would you take these home and put them in the trash for me? Or burn them."

"Shannon!" Claire protested. "Are you sure?"

"Yes. It's time. That's not my life anymore. There's nothing in that box but lies, deception, manipulation, and crushed dreams." She gave it a little shove with her foot. "And selfishness and evil. Yes, evil. Anyone who could do what he's done has an evil heart. He only thinks about himself and his desires. He didn't care at all about the pain he's caused. That he's *still* causing."

"Please, Claire. Take it out of here." She sat down, her shoulders slumped in defeat. "I don't think I ever knew the real Andrew."

Claire took the box to her car and returned. "Well, this chapter of your life is closed, but it's not the end of the book, Shannon. You'll make it through to the next one, and it will be much happier."

"I know. One of the things Dad told me was not to let Andrew change me, not to give him that power. I try to think about that when I feel myself getting bitter or when I'm feeling sorry for myself or wanting revenge. I know this sounds awful, but sometimes I've actually wished for something bad to happen to Andrew, as payback. But I know where those thoughts come from, so I don't give in to them. That doesn't help the pain though. It's going to be really hard when his baby is here."

"Remember when we were younger, we used to drown our tears in popcorn and soda? Let's escape reality for a few hours. Does this little town have a movie theater?"

"No, but there's one about thirty minutes away."

"Okay—what do you say, time for a movie? Just like old times."

"Sure. I need a distraction." They ended the evening with the movie and another long talk before bed. It was good to be together again.

After a brisk jog together around the lake the next morning, they ate breakfast, talking about everything but Claire's news. Finally, Claire announced it was time she got on the road. They said their goodbyes, both promising to check in more often than they had.

Loneliness followed Shannon back to the apartment, only now it was compounded by a greater sense of loss. There had been weeks lately when she'd barely thought of Andrew, but now he had taken up residence in her mind again, and she didn't know how to stop it.

Monday dragged by slowly. Shannon couldn't get her mind off Claire's news and her own misery. She spent her lunchbreak in her new car, trying to cheer herself up. She had to do something. She tried to pray, but she was so angry it didn't feel like her prayers would even make it past the sunroof, much less to heaven.

She remembered Carla telling her how talking to Rose at the Amaryllis had helped her cope with the loss of her mother. Maybe Rose could help her. She rifled through the console divider, sure she'd left a card from the flower shop there. Yes, there it was. She had a few more minutes before she had to be back at her desk. She dialed three times before she let the phone finish connecting, but then it rang, and Rose answered.

"The Amaryllis; this is Rose."

"Hi Rose, it's Shannon Enright. We met a few weeks ago. Could I come talk to you for a while, maybe after work sometime? When it's not busy or maybe after closing time?"

"Of course, Shannon. Why don't you stop by tonight, around five? I have two volunteers scheduled after school, and Libby can manage for me."

"Thank you." Shannon's voice showed her relief. "I'll see you then."

The shop was quiet when Shannon arrived. A few customers were visiting in the Tea Cozy, but the flower shop was empty.

Rose greeted her at the door. "Hello, dear. Would you like to go to the cottage to talk? Libby's on the register right now."

"That's probably the best place," Shannon agreed. The two women made their way through the shop and out through the garden. Rose led the way into the cottage and began bustling about in her home.

"Make yourself comfortable in the living room. I'll start a kettle for tea and be right there."

Shannon eased into a comfy chair facing the window with a view of the gardens. Brightly colored mums and a variety of pumpkin, squash, and other seasonal gourds announced the firm presence of autumn. Even with the annuals gone, the gardens were lovely.

Rose brought in the teapot and some cups and placed them on the side table. She offered one to Shannon, then settled into an antique wooden rocker near the window.

"Ahh," she sighed. "It's good to sit down, isn't it?" The chair creaked softly as she rocked. "So, what can I help you with, Shannon?"

"Gosh, Rose. I know we hardly know each other, but everyone tells me how easy you are to talk to and that you give great advice. I hope you don't mi—"

"I don't mind one bit, sweet girl. I can tell you're carrying something heavy."

"Heavy, yeah. I've been processing some emotions recently. I've had a hard time talking about it, but this weekend . . . well, everything's changed, and I don't know what to do."

"Well, whatever it is, talking will help," Rose assured her.

"Okay . . . So, I don't know if you know this, but I moved here to get away from my ex-husband's betrayal. I thought a fresh start would help me heal, and it did for a while. I love my new apartment and my job, and I've made some great friendships. I've been feeling more confident each week. I even started to believe I was going to be able to leave the past behind. But then Claire, my friend from home, she visited over the weekend and—" She stopped, blinking rapidly. She took a deep breath, determined that she wouldn't cry. She rubbed her hand roughly over her face, then blurted the words. "And she told me that Andrew—my ex—and his girlfriend are having a baby . . . and I figured out . . ." Her voice broke. "I figured out it was conceived while we were still married."

The creaking of the rocker stopped. Rose handed her a tissue.

"I feel like . . . like my heart was just starting to heal," she sobbed, "and now the scabs have been ripped right off and I'm back where I started before I moved here—or maybe worse."

"Oh, Shannon, I'm sorry. That is another painful betrayal, piled on top of the first one. I'm glad you came to talk to me, so I know exactly how to pray for you and the situation. It takes an extra measure of God's grace to cope when someone we love has been so cruel and deceptive."

"That's just it, Rose. I don't have any grace. I'm angry, really angry. *I wanted that baby.* It should be *mine!* Andrew didn't want one at first and then we couldn't and now? Yeah, there's no grace here. And you know what? I don't care. He doesn't *deserve* grace."

The older woman looked at her lovingly, without judgment. "That's okay, honey. God has enough grace for you—He can carry you through this process when you have no strength of your own. It's okay to be angry; God understands that. He wants you to bring your burdens to Him and to be honest about what you're feeling. He can heal your deepest pain because He endured the ultimate betrayal—for you and for me. And since He's all knowing, none of this has surprised Him."

"I know." Shannon took another tissue and wiped her eyes. "And I've been thinking about that recently—I'm seeing Jesus's betrayal in a different light now. He wasn't surprised by that either, but He let it happen."

"Yes. You're connecting emotionally with His betrayal and suffering now because you've had a glimpse of what He went through. And He understands your pain better than anyone else could. It's not an easy road, dear. It's a painful one. But the Lord promises He will renew our strength when we place our hope in Him. He will complete the good work that He began in your life. And He does still have good things in store for you, Shannon."

She sniffed. "I know that's what the Bible says. I'm trying to believe Him. But I'm so tired. It's a struggle to face the world some days."

Her momentous decision from that awful rainy day flashed through her mind. At least she wasn't *there* anymore. "I'm trying to stay positive, but it isn't easy."

"Give yourself some grace, dear. It's okay to acknowledge the toll this has had on your emotions. And now, you've had another painful shock. It's rocked your world once again. You are a beautiful woman with many gifts and talents. God will fulfill His plans for you as He has promised. I know you can't see very far ahead right now, but you can trust that He's still at work in your life. He's faithful that way."

"I feel like a failure," Shannon admitted, turning her head toward the window.

"Oh, dear, never think like that. Those thoughts are not from God. You have not failed. Andrew's uncaring, selfish actions were not your fault, nor are they your responsibility. Your responsibility here, before God, lies in how you deal with the painful circumstances. He doesn't want you to become bitter, and when you turn to Him, He will keep your heart tender and sensitive to His continuing guidance. Now, why don't you go wash your face, and I'll fix us something to eat."

Shannon made her way to the bathroom while Rose busied herself in the kitchen. When she returned, Rose was pulling two steaming, fragrant mugs of soup from the microwave.

"I hope you've got enough New Englander in you now to like a good corn chowder. I made this earlier today when I knew you'd be by. Thought we might need some sustenance. I've got some scones here, too."

Shannon breathed in appreciatively. "That smells marvelous. So far everything I've tasted that you've made has been wonderful. I can't wait. And your scones are the best."

"Thank you. I use my grandmother's recipes. She was Scottish and always claimed the Scots made the best scones. My British friends tend to disagree." She winked.

"My grandmother was British—you remind me of her, very wise and caring. I have her Staffordshire china teacups and always think of her when I use them."

"That's a sweet compliment, dear. Now, would it be okay if I prayed for you before we eat?"

Tears sprang to Shannon's eyes again, but she pushed them back. "Please," she murmured. "I need that very much."

Rose and Shannon bowed their heads, and Rose asked God to

heal the scars in Shannon's heart, impart His strength and hope to her, and bless her each day.

"Thank you, Rose. You're a wonderful encouragement. You've helped me see things more clearly. I know it will still be hard for a long time, but I'm trying to be more hopeful."

"We can always have hope, my dear, when we keep our eyes on the Lord."

"That's true." Shannon enjoyed another spoonful of chowder, then reached out to admire the large pink and white amaryllis that sat in the center of the table. "This plant is gorgeous. So many blooms. It's looks like your pin. Is it the same variety?"

"Mmm hmm. It's one of my favorites—very stately, sometimes grows up to two feet tall with six to eight blossoms on each stem. I've had this bulb for several years, and the blossoms are more beautiful every time it blooms."

"It truly is a striking display." Shannon turned the pot slowly so she could observe each blossom. "I'm curious, though, why you decided to name your shop the Amaryllis."

"Well, there are some interesting facts about the amaryllis that were an inspiration for the shop's name. The original Greek word means 'sparkling.' The Victorians associated the flower with strength, confidence, and determination. My late husband informed me of that when he presented me with this pin." She gently patted the pink and white flower pinned over her heart. A delicate blush painted her cheeks as she continued. "He told me I had those qualities. Of course, I know he was biased. Nevertheless, I have appreciated the association with such admirable qualities. Wearing my pin every day reminds me to strive to be worthy of his assessment."

"Oh, I think you are. You're strong and confident. You're an inspiration, too."

"Well, thank you, my dear. Have you ever seen an amaryllis bulb after the blossoms have faded?"

"No, I don't think I have. The ones you have in the shop are at various stages of blooming."

"Excuse me, dear. I'll be right back." She jumped up and left the room for a brief moment. When she returned, she was carrying a dry, brown bulb with short crusty protrusions where previous stalks had been cut off. She handed the bulb to Shannon. "Not very pretty is it? Pretty unsightly actually."

"Hard to imagine such beautiful blooms coming from this. It looks dead." She touched one of the protrusions, and it fell off the bulb.

"It's far from dead. It's just dormant, storing up energy for the next flowering cycle—and most often the new flowers will be bigger and more abundant than the last cycle's were. Isn't that a lot like us? We have to go through periods of refreshing—trials and difficulties—so we can bloom brightly once again."

Shannon set the bulb on the table next to the potted one. "There's a great lesson here, isn't there? I kinda feel like this ugly bare bulb right now. I'm not blooming . . . I'm just trying to survive. Honestly, right now I feel like maybe I'll never bloom again. Not soon . . . or ever."

"We all feel that way at times." Rose picked up the bulb again. "This bulb has everything inside it that it needs to bloom. And God has placed everything in your heart that *you* need to bloom beautifully again. It's part of our created DNA, so to speak. We're more resilient than we realize, especially when we trust in the strength of the Lord."

Shannon shook her head, glancing at the potted plant again. "I'll never look at an amaryllis the same way. Now I understand why you wear your pin every day—it's very special. I'm sorry it got damaged. How did that happen?"

"Oh, that's a story for another time, dear. I don't treasure it any less because it was damaged. I enjoy the daily reminder of who gave it to me and why."

"Well, now it's a reminder for me too. Thank you for telling me all that."

"You're welcome, Shannon. I enjoy talking with you. I see a spark in you that you may not even recognize yet."

They finished their soup and scones, then walked back to the shop. Rose relieved Libby at the register, and Shannon headed straight for the Tea Cozy. She found an empty thankfulness table, where she sat down, made a few notations on the tablecloth, then signed her initials and the date.

She was feeling much lighter as she made her way to the front of the store. She stopped to give Rose a hug on her way out.

"Thank you so much, Rose. I can't tell you how much help you've been."

"You come by any time you need to talk, dear. And don't worry—I'll be talking to Jesus about you. He has a wonderful hope and a future for you."

Shannon left the shop with a teary smile on her face.

Chapter Six 🌹

On the drive home the next afternoon, she thought about the puppy again. She did need a companion. She made a quick call to the shelter to confirm the puppy was still available. It was, so Shannon made an appointment for after work on Wednesday. Then she stopped by a pet store for puppy necessities.

On Wednesday, the excitement of bringing the pup home helped keep her mind off Andrew. She wasn't ready to tell anyone what was going on yet, but she couldn't wait to get to the shelter. When the adoption paperwork and purchase were completed, the puppy—whom she promptly christened Willow—bounded into Shannon's waiting arms and covered her with exuberant, wet kisses. The dog didn't resist the collar or leash and eagerly jumped into the back seat of Shannon's car.

She drove home with the puppy behind her and a giant smile on her face. She couldn't wait to tell Jen that she'd adopted her puppy's sibling. Clark would be so happy, she was sure.

Shannon showed Willow to the crate in her apartment and

went downstairs to pay the pet deposit at the office. When she returned, she found the pup sleeping soundly. "We need each other, don't we, girl?" she whispered. "Good night, Willow."

Shannon was dreading the undeniable signs of impending winter: the absence of warm days, the holiday decorations and sales popping up. It wasn't yet December, but the Christmas season was already making itself known. It had been her favorite time of year, but now she sensed depression creeping in and worked hard to resist the mental images of happy families and holiday get-togethers and . . . and Andrew's coming baby.

Advice she'd been given, lines she'd heard—she repeated them often to herself. *Play the cards you're dealt. This may seem like the end of the world right now, but it isn't. It's a new beginning. Don't let him change who you are; don't give him that power.* But no matter how many times she said them, they didn't bring relief.

She tried to focus on the blessings of her new life—her job, the apartment, and her new friends; yet as the weeks passed, she struggled with the frequent rush of sadness and discouragement. She kept up a strong front at work and on the phone with her parents, but at home she was insecure and heartbroken.

There were dark days when even Willow couldn't help with her depression, but overall, the dog was proving to be a great companion. Most Sunday afternoons they spent outside on the trails and around the lake, while Shannon trained her in manners and obedience. One trail followed the river all the way to the center of town, past an old grist mill, some farms, and numerous barns. Centuries-old weathered stone walls, still intact, delineated property lines and lined dirt roads. Almost to her surprise at times, Shannon found herself enjoying her little piece of country paradise.

And at night, back in the quiet of the apartment, they slept side by side. She didn't mind the doggy snores; they were company in an otherwise lonely world.

One Friday night in early December, she met Carla and another coworker, Sarah, for dinner in town. It wasn't the same as hanging out with Claire, but she was enjoying these new friends. After dinner, Carla suggested they head to the Amaryllis.

"I need to pick up a birthday gift there," she said. "You guys want to come along?"

"Always." Sarah replied. "I love that place."

Shannon's heart felt light as she followed Carla and Sarah into the flower shop. She hadn't realized how much she'd missed the place, and she admired the holiday décor, new since the last time she'd visited.

They found Rose at a table in the Tea Cozy, seated across from a man who appeared to be taking notes. "Hi girls," she called. "Max and I are a little busy right now, but you let me know if you need anything."

"Okay, we're browsing." Carla replied, looking through a section of note cards. "These are perfect." She held up a box of cards covered with photos of poppies. "This is for my sister. Now I need a bouquet for her."

"Shannon, have you met Max?" Sarah whispered, her eyes twinkling.

"No."

"He's our town's most eligible bachelor. He's a reporter for the local paper and a great guy." Sarah needed to learn how to whisper more . . . whispery.

Shannon tried to check him out nonchalantly, but he turned his head toward her at the same time, and their eyes met momentarily. *Wow, he's handsome.* She looked away quickly and joined Carla at the counter where Libby was preparing some fresh poppies and a vase. Rose walked to the register, and Max followed behind.

Sarah didn't hesitate. "Max, this is my new friend, Shannon. She works at Stark and is a New York transplant," she announced.

"Hello, Shannon. Happy to meet you; welcome to Connecticut." His clear blue eyes looked piercingly through hers, and his wide smile was charming.

A frisson of awareness ran up her spine, and she tried not to shiver.

"Glad to meet you also." Her polite response belied her inner turmoil. *Obviously a ladies' man,* she thought as she followed Sarah to the door. *That's enough of you.*

"So? What do you think? Isn't he handsome?" Sarah asked on the way to the car.

"Not interested. He looks like the type who has a girlfriend in every town." *And I'm not blushing.*

"No, not Max," Carla protested. "He's a genuine guy. A friend of mine dated him for a few months, and he was a perfect gentleman. I told her she was crazy to break up with him, but she found some musician in Shelton."

Shannon laughed and shook her head. "Nope. I'm perfectly happy with my new dog. She's all the company I need right now. The thought of dating is frightening, unimaginable actually." *That's all I need—another man in the mix.*

She couldn't move past the one she'd had.

Claire visited again, a few weeks before Andrew's baby was due. Shannon couldn't help it—she burst into tears before Claire could finish asking how she was doing.

"I'm glad you're here," she cried. "You're the only one I can really talk to about what I'm feeling. I mean, I've talked to one lady in town, but . . . you're the only one who understands everything.

"I'm not handling things well now at all; seems like I've reversed all the progress I made. It's so stupid—I'm miles away. He's completely moved on, but here I am—can't stop thinking about the house, the dreams for the future I thought we shared. The lies, the double life, his insensitivity, betrayal . . . it's a lot. But adding the baby into all this is too much . . ." She tried unsuccessfully to stop the tears. "It's just too much; I can't handle it."

"I know, Shannon. Mark and I don't understand either; we thought we knew Andrew well, but obviously, we didn't. But you aren't going to let any of this change you. You're the same person you always were."

"Nothing helps the pain. And it's only going to be worse when his baby gets here. This is supposed to be my baby, *our baby*, not *hers*."

They talked until late that night. An early Saturday morning walk along the lake wore Willow out. Instead of making breakfast, Shannon suggested a drive to Rose's for tea and pastries.

"You'll love Rose. Her shop is a fave of most people in town—really unique. She's the one I've talked to a little too."

Following an introduction at the floral counter, they sat at a thankfulness table in the Tea Cozy. Shannon jotted down a few things on the tablecloth she was thankful for, then added her initials and the date. She knew focusing on being thankful—for something, anything—would help reset her perspective. Claire jotted a few things down too, then filled out a note card, folded it in half, and placed it in a basket on the table labeled "prayer requests."

When she looked up, she caught Shannon's questioning gaze. She shrugged. "I didn't want to tell you earlier because of everything you've been going through. Umm, Mark and I—well, I miscarried a few months ago. I wasn't very far along," she added quickly, fighting back tears. "We're going to try again soon. Mark took it pretty hard too."

"Claire! Oh, I wish I would have known." Shannon reached

over and gave her friend a hug. "You've been such a huge help and comfort for me. And at the same time I was complaining. I'm so sorry. I feel bad I wasn't there for you. What can I do now?"

"You know I miscarried a year ago too, so when this one came along, we didn't tell many people about it. I'm glad now. Mark and I have decided if I don't get pregnant again in a year, we'll adopt. I don't think I can go through another miscarriage. We don't want to wait too much longer to start a family, though."

Shannon nodded understandingly. "The unknowns in life are so hard to deal with. I will pray you get pregnant again soon without any complications."

"Thanks. Our parents are so anxious to have grandchildren," she sighed. "There's a lot of pressure. And I really do want to be a mom."

Once they'd finished their pastries, Claire and Shannon browsed awhile in the floral shop. A sky-blue vase on display behind the checkout counter caught Claire's attention.

"Shannon, look! That vase is gorgeous. But I think it's been broken."

"Yeah, most everything in here has." Shannon laughed. "But Rose makes them beautiful again."

"Really? That's . . . different. But look at this one. I think there's gold in the cracks."

Rose joined them, a bright smile on her face. "It is gold. A friend gave me that vase after a trip to Japan. She thought I should try the technique. It's a Japanese art form called *kintsugi*. It's also called golden repair. The artist mixes lacquer with powdered gold and then mends the broken areas of the pottery. The purpose is to accent the repair instead of disguising it. Some people refer to it as the art of precious scars. The end result is often more beautiful than the original, I think. This vase is what gave me the idea of repairing broken items in my shop." She laughed and gestured to the other shelves. "And now it's a hobby that keeps growing, as you can see."

"I do see. What a beautiful story, Rose." Claire said.

"Thank you. When I repair a broken item, I say a prayer for the person who will eventually receive it. We all have precious scars from brokenness, but we're never beyond restoration."

"That's true. And what a wonderful thing to do." Claire picked up a teacup on display nearby. "Look at this one, Shannon. It's gorgeous. That delicate spray of lilacs, and this little line of gold . . . not original, but I can't imagine the cup without it."

"It is pretty, isn't it," Shannon said, her eyes on Rose. Claire set the cup down and wandered off. Shannon quickly handed it and her credit card to Rose, a conspiratorial finger to her lips. Rose's eyes twinkled as she rang up the purchase and placed it in a box. Shannon managed to drop it into her handbag just as Claire came back around.

"Rose, your shop is absolutely delightful," she gushed. "If I lived closer, I would be here all the time."

"Well, please come, whenever you're visiting. It was nice to meet you, Claire."

"I certainly will visit again." Claire gave Rose a hug as they left the store.

In the car, Claire started to cry. "I feel like I'm broken right now. There's a huge hole in my heart . . . I'm so completely sad. I loved our babies, even if it was only for a few months. We named them, you know. Ethan and Marie."

"Oh, Claire. I'm so sorry. Why does life have to be so hard?" Shannon hesitated a moment, then drew the little box out of her bag. "I was going to wait to give you this, maybe for Christmas, but I think you need it now."

Claire took the box with shaky fingers and opened it. She gasped when she saw the teacup. "How? Why? I mean, thank you, Shannon. It's beautiful, but—"

Shannon gave her a quick side hug. "We're both broken right now, Claire," she said. "But it's like Rose says, God can make broken things beautiful. Without all our cracks and chips, we'd just be perfect little people who might or might not honor Him." She laughed. "I'm kind of preaching to myself too . . . but doesn't it say somewhere in Job about God refining us through fire, and we'll be like gold? So, maybe He's got some gold to fill the cracks around your broken heart."

Claire traced the thin gold line on the little teacup. "Maybe."

Sunday morning after Claire left, Shannon found herself overwhelmed with sadness, both for herself and for Claire and Mark. She simply couldn't understand why God was allowing so much pain in their lives. It wasn't fair that Claire and Mark had lost two babies, but Andrew and that woman were going to have one in a few weeks.

Willow, who always sensed when Shannon was feeling down, nudged in close and let out a gentle *woof*. It was the catalyst Shannon needed to get up and go outside. Within minutes, she had her shoes and coat on and was heading out with Willow on her leash. The fresh air, coupled with soulful looks and sighs from her puppy, helped turn Shannon's mood in the right direction.

To avoid another lonely afternoon, Shannon wandered into town again and stopped at the Amaryllis. Rose was swamped with new orders and customers. "Rose, it looks like you could use some help. Is there something I can do?"

"I'll never turn away a helping hand, dear, especially with Christmas a couple of weeks away. Thanks. Would you mind ringing out some customers so I can finish up a few orders?"

Shannon found she enjoyed the interaction with Rose's customers, and realized her mood had picked up significantly. *Hmm, I wonder if I could volunteer here for a few hours on the weekends.*

When there was a lull, Shannon asked Rose.

"Dear, you're a godsend. I was talking to the Lord last week-end about needing more help." She brushed back a few strands of gray hair that had separated from her bun. "Being busy is a good problem to have, you know, but I really can't afford extra staff right now."

"That's not a problem. I would love to volunteer. I could come in for a few hours on Saturdays—I know that's your busiest day."

"Perfect. Either mornings or afternoons, whichever fits your schedule."

Shannon began early the next Saturday, working at the register and greeting customers. She hadn't seen many men in her visits to the Amaryllis, so she was surprised when a middle-aged man came in, leading a young woman who was visibly upset. He stopped at the register.

"Hello, I'm Pastor Dalton. I don't believe I've seen you here before."

"Yes, I'm Shannon. I started helping out today."

"I'm happy to meet you, Shannon. This is Danielle. We're here to see Rose; she's expecting us."

"I believe she's in the Tea Cozy area."

"Okay, thank you." Shannon watched the young woman surreptitiously wipe away tears as she followed the pastor to the tea-room. *Interesting.*

Filling orders and checking out customers made the morning pass quickly. Shannon was surprised when Rose came to relieve her at 11:00. She was also curious.

"Was that girl who came in with the pastor okay?" she asked.

"Danielle? She's going through some hard stuff right now. She'll be staying with me for a few weeks. She's offered to help with cleaning the shop and my cottage, which I will appreciate very much. I'm so glad you were here today. It gave me some extra time to spend with her."

"Of course. I'll be back next Saturday."

Chapter Seven

Christmas and New Year's came and went with little notice. She put in extra hours at the Amaryllis, which gave her a little Christmas spirit, but otherwise, it was easier to ignore the holidays than dwell on what should have been. She declined her parents' invitation to come home for the holiday week, pointing out that she didn't have vacation time yet at work. They were disappointed.

Life was finally settling back into a normal routine, and Shannon was glad. One Thursday afternoon on her drive home from work, her phone rang. She was surprised to see her mom's number in the display. "Mom? Hi! What's up?"

"Hey, sweetie. Dad and I were wondering if you could come home this weekend."

"Umm . . . maybe. I'm still volunteering at the flower shop in town though. I'd have to make sure she can get someone else in." She hesitated. "Is everything okay?"

"Oh, sure. We're fine. We just miss you. Thought it'd be nice to see you and meet your little dog."

"That would be nice. Let me talk to Rose. I'll call you back in a few."

On the phone, Rose assured her she had all the help she needed, so she took Friday off. Shannon loaded Willow and a suitcase into her car and headed home.

They arrived late that evening. Shannon's parents met her at the door with Coop, their dog. He and Willow, fast friends, tumbled out into the yard to burn off energy.

They gathered in the sunroom the next morning for breakfast, enjoying Mom's homemade biscuits and fresh brewed coffee. The dogs provided joyful entertainment as they frolicked in the backyard.

Shannon snuggled down between her parents on the long sofa. She sighed with contentment. "You were right, Mom. It is good to be home. I missed you both."

"We missed you too. I'm glad Claire was able to visit you, even though we couldn't yet."

"Me too. Did you hear what happened to her?"

"To Claire? No, what?"

"She said I could tell you. She and Mark lost another baby. Right before Christmas."

"Aww, that poor girl," Mom said, sympathy in her eyes. "I'll add them to my prayer list."

"Umm . . ." Dad cleared his throat and shifted uncomfortably. "Honey, we wanted you to come home this weekend because we needed to talk to you. In person."

Shannon sat up. "It's Andrew isn't it? Their baby's due any day, right? Is it here?"

"Yes." Mom picked up her hand and rubbed it. "We didn't want you to be alone when you heard. Claire called me on Thursday. Apparently Andrew sent Mark an email announcement on Wednesday."

Shannon drew a deep breath. "Did he marry her?"

"No. I asked Mark the same thing."

Shannon sniffled. "Is it a girl or a boy?"

"A girl. Sienna."

Eyes dry, Shannon stood up. "Thanks for telling me and for being concerned. I'm glad I came home. There's no place I'd rather be this weekend than here with you two." She finished her coffee and carried her mug to the kitchen.

"I think I'm going to take Willow out for a while. Since it's a sunny day, we'll go to Hyde Lake. I'm okay—I just need some time to process this."

She gathered her dog and her car keys, coat, and a backpack, and headed out the door.

She recalled how Rose had encouraged her to resist self-pity. She had been trying, but it seemed impossible now.

Hyde Lake was one of Shannon's favorite spots, a healing place she had visited often before moving to Connecticut. The well-maintained walking trail wound around the lake, dotted with wooden benches and observation binoculars for wildlife viewing. She found an isolated sunny bench halfway around the lake and sat down. Willow sniffed at the bare bushes behind her. A sudden rush of wings startled both of them, and Shannon turned around to see a great blue heron—blue-gray wings spread wide, pencil-thin legs dangling behind—rise from a nearby tree. Willow barked, and a smaller heron joined the first in the air. Shannon focused her binoculars on the top of the tree and was delighted to see a large nest propped among the boughs.

"Look, Willow, a male, a female, and their nest . . . a family." *A family!* Sudden tears streamed down her cheeks. She couldn't even escape the painful images in the middle of the woods.

"Oh God, will this pain ever go away?" The words came from deep within her broken spirit. She coaxed Willow up onto the bench beside her and began stroking her soft fur. Brushing the tears off her cheeks, she pulled a journal out of her backpack and began writing. Anger, pain, doubts, disillusionment, lost love . . . the words flew off her pen. Before long, the thoughts became prayer, and she began speaking aloud.

"Lord, I don't understand why this has happened. I trusted You. I believed my marriage was forever, that our love would be forever. And I know I've been angry with You—but You let this happen. I know everyone has free will, and Andrew made his choice. I'm sorry. I don't want to be tied up in this self-pity. I don't want to become bitter. Please, forgive me. I need Your help just to make it through a day. I need Your peace and hope. Help me, Lord. Please help me." After a while, she stood and began walking again, Willow faithfully at her side.

When she returned, neither Mom nor Dad asked any questions; they respectfully gave her the space she needed. Dad did give her a hug, though, and said, "We were thinking about going out for dinner. Murphy's Kitchen has a new chef. Want to go?"

"Oh, I haven't had Murphy's for so long. It sounds great. Do they still serve shepherd's pie? You know it's my favorite."

"You bet, and it's still as good as ever."

"Okay. Let me freshen up a bit, and I'll be right down."

"Take your time. I'll make reservations for six-thirty."

The shepherd's pie did not disappoint, and Andrew's name was not mentioned again. It felt good to laugh at her dad's jokes, just like old times.

Sunday was a different story, however. She hadn't been to church since before she'd left home, and it took some courage to go back. She was sure people would be whispering and judging her, but instead, the welcome she received warmed her heart.

At least Andrew wasn't there. She'd been worried about that.

Not that he'd have been there with a brand-new baby, anyway, but—she stopped the thought there.

After church and a leisurely lunch with her parents, she packed up her car and her dog. Mom and Dad walked her out as she prepared to leave.

"Shannon, we're so proud of you," Dad said, giving her a firm hug. "You're showing a great deal of courage and resilience in difficult circumstances. Keep trusting God to know what's best for you. He's not going to let this pain go to waste."

"I know, Dad. I'm trying hard to do that. And I'm not giving Andrew the power to change me. Thank you for speaking that truth into me. It's been my anchor more times than you can know."

The conversation stayed with her for a good part of the drive back to Loughton Valley. It wasn't easy to believe that God could bring any good out of the mess she was in—but she was determined to try. He promised she could trust Him.

"I could use some of Your hope now, Lord."

Chapter Eight

Shannon was at the shop early the next Saturday morning, helping Rose ready the custom orders for the day. They had only just unlocked the door when the bell overhead announced a visitor.

Rose greeted him cheerily, and Shannon looked up to find Max striding their way.

"Hi, Rose." He gave her a quick hug, then turned to Shannon.

"Good morning. You're Shannon, right?"

The man's smile could light a fire. *But not mine.*

"Yes. And you're Max. We met here a month or so ago."

"We did, and I've been meaning to ask if you'd like to go out for coffee some time. I know you're still new to the area. Maybe we could explore the town a bit?" He raised an eyebrow, drawing her attention to startlingly blue eyes.

Is he asking me for a date? Well, what if he is? She looked down at the counter for a moment, then gathered her courage. Even if he was only being neighborly, she was surprised to find she was intrigued. She'd do it!

She raised her chin and smiled back at the man. "I get off work here at eleven."

"That'd be great. I'll be back then." He waved as he left, but his presence lingered in the air, a spicy scent that Shannon couldn't identify.

She busied herself nervously, already regretting her decision. Rose watched her for a few moments, then came over to where she stood. She gathered Shannon's hands in hers.

"Look at me, Shannon. It's okay."

Shannon drew a shaky breath.

"Max is a good guy. He has a great reputation, and I've found him to be quite trustworthy."

"I'm sure he is, but I don't think I'm ready to date yet. Just thinking about that is overwhelming."

"Well, it's just coffee in the middle of the day. You could stay here at the Tea Cozy if you want." She laughed as she glanced toward the tearoom. "It gets a little busy in there around eleven, though, and Max is quite a guy. You might not get much privacy."

Rose had a point. Shannon wasn't sure what she wanted.

Max returned at 10:50, and Shannon was ready. She marked her timesheet and gathered her coat. She'd decided against the Tea Cozy when Sarah and Carla walked in. Date or not, she didn't want to hear about it on Monday.

As she came around the counter, Max said, "Shannon, I know we said coffee, and that's still okay if you'd like, but it's so close to lunchtime. Have you been to the café on the square? We could have lunch together there if that sounds good." *Ugh, that smile, and those bright blue eyes!*

Shannon hesitated for a moment, then took the plunge. "Sure. We could do that. My friend Jen says the café is great, but I haven't been there yet. That would be nice. Thank you."

Max helped her with her coat, and they headed out into the

brisk air. Surprisingly, Max was easy to talk to, and Shannon found her nervousness melting away. They reached the café and went in. A waitress seated them right away.

Shannon opened her menu. "Any recommendations?" she asked.

"Their burgers are amazing."

By the time the waitress returned to the table, she was ready to order. "I'll try the avocado burger, please."

Max added his order, the big beef with bacon and cheddar. Then he began the conversation by asking how she liked her job and Loughton Valley. He was very engaging; he had great eye contact and was a good listener. She was surprised to find she enjoyed talking with him. But enough about her. It was time to change the subject.

"So I heard you're a reporter."

"Sort of a jack-of-all-trades with the local paper. Most of our business is online now, but we still crank out a weekly. I used to work for a larger paper in Bridgeport, but I like the smaller town papers better; much easier to connect with people. I mostly write local news stories, cover sporting events, and maintain a news blog. I'm writing a series of articles now about shop owners on the square. I was interviewing Rose the evening I met you. We're meeting again next week."

The d-word came up later in their conversation; Max introduced it. He explained he had been married for four years, until he discovered his wife was having an affair with a state representative in Hartford.

"I tried to make it work, even after finding out. I suggested counseling, but she wasn't interested in saving the marriage. I think she was too intrigued by his status and income, neither of which I could compete with. I wished her the best, and we parted ways."

Shannon told him briefly about her divorce but left out the

baby part. They had a lot in common, and she was impressed that Max didn't seem bitter about his situation. After lunch, they walked around the square and visited a few shops.

Before heading back to Rose's, they sat on one of the benches in the gazebo for a while. No awkward moments—conversation flowed naturally, and Shannon thoroughly enjoyed his companionship. She hoped he felt the same.

They popped in briefly to say goodbye to Rose, then Max walked Shannon to her car. "I'd like to see you again, if it's okay. I enjoyed our time together, Shannon."

"I'd like that," she responded. "I had a good time too." They exchanged phone numbers, and she realized how much she had missed male companionship. She hummed a happy tune as she drove home.

Willow greeted her at the door, and Shannon grabbed the leash and took her out.

"Hey, girl," she said cheerily. "I met a really nice guy today." As they walked, she told the dog about her new friend. When she realized what she was doing, she laughed at herself and headed back inside. She hung up her coat and settled on the couch with her laptop. Feeling a little guilty, she typed his name into a Google search bar. *Maxwell Harrington.* Information about several journalism awards he had received, both in Bridgeport and Loughton Valley, popped up right away. *Impressive.*

Shannon jumped when her phone rang. She looked at the display, relieved to see it was Jen. She answered with a smile on her face. "Jen. Hi. Haven't seen you in a few days. What's up?"

Jennifer laughed. "Girl, is there something you need to tell me? I swear I saw you and Maxwell Harrington sitting in the gazebo when I drove by the square today."

"You saw us? Can't keep anything secret in this town, can we?"

Jen was silent for a moment, until Shannon laughed. "I'm kidding, Jen. You're a hoot. We had lunch together. I met him at Rose's. How long have you known him?"

"Kevin met him shortly after we moved here. He's pretty well known in town. So, are you planning to go out with him again?"

"I think so. He mentioned it, but we haven't set a date or anything. What's Kevin's impression of him?"

"I think Kev would say Max is well respected. Why don't you come over for dinner and you can ask him. We're grilling chicken."

"Oh, that sounds yummy. Thanks."

During dinner, Shannon asked Kevin about his association with Max.

"He's professional, well-liked in town, active in community events. I met him at an awards ceremony a few years ago when he was being recognized for his work with local charities. So . . . were there any fireworks?" He jiggled his eyebrows at her.

Shannon laughed. "It was one brief lunch date, guys. But he was a gentleman and very engaging. It wasn't awkward like I envisioned my first date would be. Just sort of happened naturally. I met him at Rose's. He asked me out for coffee, and we ended up eating lunch together. It was fun."

"Good." Kevin stood up. "I'm going to refill my coffee. You two want anything?" Neither did, so Kevin headed toward the kitchen. In the doorway, he turned around. "The game's about to start. Anyone mind if I head to the den?"

"Of course not," Jennifer replied. "You wouldn't have stayed much longer out here anyway. We're about to have some girl talk."

Shannon couldn't help but laugh as Kevin made a quick escape after that.

"I'm happy for you, Shannon. You've got a lot to offer the world. I'm glad you're venturing out again." She stood up. "Let's get comfy in the living room, shall we?"

Once they were seated, Jennifer started talking again. "Oh, so I haven't seen you since your trip back home. How did that go?"

"It was good, Enjoyed some time with Mom and Dad. Didn't get to see Claire this time, but that's okay. Found out my ex had a baby." Her voice hardened with the last statement.

"He *what*? You haven't been divorced that long, have you?"

"No. He was unfaithful. Guess I couldn't give him one, so he decided to go make one somewhere else."

"Aww, Shannon. I'm sorry."

"It's okay. It's another part of the divorce process, I guess. Grieving what should have been, sorting out all the leftover feelings. You know, I wanted a baby so bad . . ." Her voice trailed off, and she was silent for a moment. Then she shrugged. "Anyway. I used to believe the time-heals-all-wounds line, but I don't think it's true anymore. Sorry, I didn't mean to bring down the party."

"It's okay," Jen reached over and squeezed her hand. "You know I'm here if you ever need me. I'm a good listener, even if it's four a.m."

"So you've told me." Shannon smiled at her friend. "Thanks. I'm dealing with it. I've been volunteering at Rose's. She and I talk a lot. She's helping me stay centered. There are a lot of hurting women who pass through her doors."

Jennifer nodded. "I know. And Rose gives everyone of us the individual attention we need. She always knows exactly what to say, what wisdom or encouragement each person needs to hear. She's amazing."

"She is. I don't know how she does it. And she's always busy."

"Well, I'm sure she appreciates your help at the shop."

Kevin strolled in from the den and propped himself on the arm of the couch. Jen squeezed his hand, then asked, "Does Pastor Dalton still bring girls to her occasionally?"

"Yeah, I was there when he brought one girl in. There are so many, though. I've wondered at times where she finds them." Shannon's smile was soft as she thought of her friend. "I think there are three girls in her cottage right now."

"Rose is remarkable," Kevin chimed in. "She never takes money from the women who stay with her. The churches in town have held fundraisers for beds and furniture, which is a big help. And the food pantry donates food when she needs it."

Jennifer nodded in agreement. "I remember one time, she had five girls staying with her." She shook her head. "Speaking of food, we still have dessert. I made a blueberry tart."

Shannon stayed a while longer, then headed back to her apartment. She shivered as she got Willow ready for a walk. Winter had definitely arrived. Returning to the apartment once more, she got ready for bed.

Her journal caught her eye, and she picked it up. A continual list-maker, she began jotting down all the qualities she had observed in Max. Then she added what Kevin and Jennifer and even Rose had told her. "Handsome, courteous, friendly, a gentleman, good listener, engaging, good eye contact, seems happy, well adjusted, well respected and respectful, trustworthy, good sense of humor, loves people and animals, enjoys being outdoors, successful, recognized in the community, good outlook on life, humble, mature."

She read over the list again. *I hope he calls.*

On Tuesday evening he did call, and they set a date for the weekend. Shannon thought about him often during that week, worrying that she was moving too fast and then deciding that a few dates couldn't hurt.

Max picked her up Friday evening, and they drove to the theater in Jackson. She was surprised how increasingly comfortable she felt with Max, and when he asked to spend the next day together as well, she didn't hesitate.

"I'm scheduled at the Amaryllis in the morning, but I can be done there by eleven."

"What would you like to do?" he asked. "We could hit the snowshoe trails in Osbornedale State Park, go ice skating at the Milford Pavilion, or we could take a drive to Yale and maybe explore a few of the museums in New Haven. Or anything else you'd rather do."

"I've never been to Yale. I've heard the old buildings there are beautiful."

"They are. Yale was founded in 1701—I wrote an article about its history two years ago. I think I could find my way back to a great Italian restaurant nearby too."

"It's a date—sounds like a fun day."

The sun was bright and the sky cloudless with no chance of snow when Max picked her up from Rose's at 11:00. The drive was quick, only twenty minutes. Again, Shannon marveled at how easy Max was to talk to. Today he wanted to know about her past.

"Are you a native New Yorker?"

"No, I was born in Columbia, Pennsylvania—a little town near Lancaster in Amish country. My paternal grandfather had a farm there, and when Dad and Mom were first married, they lived nearby so Dad could help out with the farm. Gradually, Grandpa Sweeney sold off most of his land, so Dad found a job in Middleton. That's where I grew up. I had a lot of fun with the animals at Grandpa's farm, especially the baby lambs and goats in the spring. But I never could get used to the goat's milk Grandma always served." Shannon laughed.

"Oooph, I'm not a fan either." Max shuddered. "So is your heritage Irish?"

"Yeah, my dad's parents were Irish and English. My mom's parents were mostly from England, but from what I've heard, she has relatives in Ireland too. Never been to either country, though I'd love to go someday."

Before long, they had arrived. Max drove the perimeter of the campus, giving her a quick view. "Do you mind if we park and walk around?" he asked. "It's not too cold today."

"Sure, that's fine."

Max was at her side before she'd climbed out of the car. He took her hand and began pointing out details as they wandered among the buildings.

"Did you attend here?" Shannon asked. "You seem to know a lot about the campus."

"No, too rich for my blood," he said with a smile. "I interviewed several department heads for the article, so I'm familiar with some of the buildings."

"Are you getting hungry?" Max asked as they reached the end of the campus tour. "The Italian restaurant is only twenty minutes away. Then, if we still have time, maybe we can visit a couple museums."

"That would be perfect."

It was a full, enjoyable day. Shannon didn't want it to end, but time with Max seemed to fly. She loved how attentive and engaging he was—a stark comparison with Andrew, who had always been distracted and self-absorbed.

The fact that Max was so darn handsome was a great bonus.

Chapter Nine 🥀

Shannon walked out of work on Friday with a bright smile on her face. In her mind's eye, she was rifling through her closet, choosing what to wear. She and Max were going to Bridgeport tonight, where he was going to show her around his hometown.

She looked up as she neared her car, then froze. A familiar figure stood there, waiting for her. Chills ran up her spine, and she gasped for air. Her cheeks felt suddenly hot, and her thoughts ran in wild circles. *It can't be! Why is he here? And why does he look so good?*

"An—Andrew?" Her voice shook for a moment, but she willed herself to be strong. "No. I don't know what you're doing here, but you need to leave. Now."

"Hey, Shannon. It's okay—I just want to talk to you." His eyes traced her form, and her pulse picked up again. "You look wonderful. Please, can we go somewhere to talk?" His voice was soft and beckoning and . . . and it scared her to death.

"No. Leave. *Now!*"

"Okay, just give me five minutes. We can go someplace else if you're not comfortable talking here."

"I have nothing to say to you. And how did you find me? One of your techy-hacker friends? This is creepy."

"Please, Shannon, five minutes. Then I promise I'll leave. Baby, I made a horrible mistake. Please listen to me."

"*Baby?*" Anything warm left inside her turned to icy fury. "How dare you? And a mistake? That's what you call adultery and betrayal—a *mistake*? Like, what? You forgot to lock the door or something?"

He took a step back, his eyes wide at her reaction. It didn't stop him though. "Look, I know I've wronged you terribly. Nothing I can say will ever make things right, I know that. I messed up both our lives."

"Really? Well, I thought you were so happy with your new family." She couldn't help the mocking tone that oozed through her voice.

He reached out, but she pushed his hand away. "I'm not talking to you, Andrew."

"Shannon, I want a chance to prove to you that I've changed. I realize now I can't live without you. I've been so stupid. I don't deserve a second chance with you—I know that. But I want you to know that I still love you and I always have loved you. You are my soulmate. I'm only asking you to give me a chance," he pleaded. "Hear me out, please."

"Not likely," she snorted. "You used up your chances, Andrew, way back in July. Now move out of my way. Go home and leave me alone." She opened the car door and jumped in. The door almost caught Andrew's fingers as she slammed it shut. With a twist of the key, her car roared to life, and she threw it into gear. Good thing Andrew was quick, or she'd have run him over too.

She drove hard, watching to be sure he wasn't following her. It didn't take long, however, for the nerves to take over. Shaking and crying, she pulled into a parking lot and stopped the car. *What just happened? And why?* Memories flashed through her mind—happy ones, sad ones, painful ones.

"Why, God," she shouted. "*Why?!* I've been praying for peace. He doesn't get to do this. He doesn't. It isn't fair." She finished on a whisper.

Eventually, she made it home and took Willow out for her walk. Then she called Jen. "Hey, Jen. It's not four a.m., but I sure need a friend. Can I come over?"

"Sure, honey. Bring Willow—Clark would love the company. Kevin's still at work."

"Thanks."

Jen answered the door, her eyes widening as she took in Shannon's tearstained appearance. "What on earth, Shannon? What's happened?"

"Andrew's in town. He came to my work." Through tears, she described the encounter with her ex. "I don't understand. I'm so confused. He has a baby—he's a father. He made his choice and started a new life, and I was trying to start mine. Why is he here?"

"Jeez, I don't know what to say. What a terrible shock."

"My head is spinning. When I first saw him standing by my car, it was like, he was the man I loved. And when he spoke, he seemed sincere, but the words coming out of his mouth were crazy. I can't make sense of any of it. He and his girlfriend probably had a big fight, and he thinks he can come crawling back to me? That's a joke. I'm not that stupid. Does he actually think I'm that stupid?"

"Who knows what he's thinking. This is bizarre. You need to decide what you're going to do if he shows up here. Do you think he followed you? Does he have your phone number?"

"I don't think he followed me. I slammed out of there, and I didn't see his car. Besides, he was still walking away when I pulled out. I don't think he has my new number or address. I don't know who'd give it to him. Then again, I didn't dream he'd know where I was working, either. I can't believe he drove this far to show up without warning—" She was shaking, now with a bit of anger. "The jerk should be home caring for his baby, if nothing else."

Willow, sensing Shannon's distress, moved away from frolicking with Clark and came to sit at her feet. Shannon wrapped her arms around her and stroked her head. "Good girl, Willow. You're my buddy."

Suddenly, she sat up, her eyes wide. "Oh no! I'm a mess, and Max is going to be here at six. We're supposed to be going out tonight. Maybe I should cancel."

"I don't know, Shan," Jennifer protested. "I think it might be good to get out and get your mind off what happened. Besides, then you won't be home if Andrew does show up."

"I suppose, but what if I can't keep it together? I don't want to ruin Max's evening."

Jennifer laughed. "If you cancel, *his* night'll be ruined. I've seen the way he looks at you." She reached over and hugged her friend. "I'm kidding. No, if he cares about you the way I think he does, he'd want to be with you right now. And he'd want to know that Andrew showed up unannounced."

"But I haven't told him everything yet. I sure didn't tell him about the baby. It's humiliating and a lot of information to process all at once."

"Trust your intuition; you have a lot of wisdom."

"Well, thanks," she said dryly, "but I've been pretty lacking in that area recently. Maybe you're right. I guess I will stay with the plans for tonight. Thanks for talking me down. You're a good friend." She gathered Willow, hugged Jen, and made her way back to her apartment. She didn't see any unfamiliar cars in the lot, so she figured Andrew hadn't found where she lived.

She barely had time to freshen up and change her clothes before the doorbell rang. Max peered around a vase full of carnations from Rose's.

"You are lovely, Shannon." While she didn't fully believe him, his words warmed her heart. She stepped back to let him in and nearly tripped over Willow who was anxious to greet him as well.

"These are beautiful, Max. Thank you. I actually saw that vase at Rose's yesterday. I was admiring the beautiful colors and her kintsugi-like golden repairs. I love it." She took the arrangement and set it on the counter between the kitchen and living room.

Max bent to give Willow a belly rub. The dog flopped on her back, taking in every ounce of attention. Finally he looked up again. "Rose explained kintsugi when I brought it to the register. She said this would be a good choice. I'm glad you like it—it caught my eye right away."

He stood and put his arm around Shannon. "I'm looking forward to trying the new seafood restaurant—a coworker went last weekend and hasn't stopped raving about it since. And I thought maybe we could walk along the ocean after dinner if it's not too cold."

"That would be wonderful." Shannon grabbed her coat and a warm scarf, put Willow in her crate, and they were on their way.

Max asked about Shannon's week, and she answered, focusing on work. After a brief overview, she asked Max how his week was.

"Not much to report—" He waggled his eyebrows at her, and she groaned.

"Really?"

He laughed. "Sorry, that's a journalist joke. Pretty much a regular week, except I did spend some time with Rose again in her shop for the article I'm writing. She gave me the history of her shop and a few other businesses that were in her building prior to hers. Of course, I'll have to research further back at the library to get the full history—her building is two hundred years old. Anyway, I'm also planning to include a photo of the owners in their shops." He shrugged. "That was kinda strange—Rose doesn't want her picture taken. She said I can use photos of the interior, but she doesn't want to be in it. I never thought she'd be camera-shy."

"Hmmm, that is surprising. She *is* the shop, so I can't imagine her not being in the picture for the article."

"Right? But she was adamant—she does not want any photos of herself. Hey, maybe I'll take the picture when you're volunteering." He winked slyly. She laughed.

Max had made reservations, so they were seated right away at a table overlooking the water. The place had a coastal décor, with muted seafoam, turquoise, and beige colors and large, framed photos of fish and fishing boats on the walls. Shannon took a deep breath, hoping she didn't appear nervous or upset.

The waitress brought menus and announced the special: a lobster and crab plate.

"That sounds great," Shannon said.

"Make that two."

During dinner, Max asked more about her job. Shannon was happy to keep the conversation light so she could make it through dinner without getting emotional. She asked which other shop owners he had interviewed and who he still needed to contact. Rose was the last one. He would schedule a final interview and photoshoot with her when he had a rough draft ready. Then he could finalize her article for the paper.

The waitress returned and asked about dessert. They settled on coffee and a cheesecake to share.

"So, what do you think? Do we have time for a stroll along the beach?"

"I would love to see the beach here."

It wasn't planned. Shannon felt so comfortable with him, walking hand in hand and enjoying the bright moonlit night and the waves lapping the beach, that it just came out.

"Max, I had a huge shock today. My ex was waiting at my car after work. I have no idea how he knew where I worked. I haven't seen him since the divorce."

Max stopped and faced Shannon, holding her hand firmly. "That's crazy! Are you okay?"

"As okay as possible, I guess." She shrugged. "His girlfriend just had a baby. His baby. I knew that, so I've been trying to adjust to it for a while now. Seeing him today was not easy."

"There's a bench up ahead, under the streetlight. Let's sit over there if you're not too cold?"

"No, I'm fine." They headed toward the bench, but didn't sit down.

Max looked at her quizzically. "So, why was he there? Did he say?"

"He didn't make much sense, and I didn't want to talk to him. I told him to leave. He wouldn't, so I got in my car and left." Shannon didn't want to repeat the actual words Andrew had spoken.

"Do you feel safe, Shannon?"

The streetlight gave enough light for her to see his genuine concern. It was a welcomed comfort. "No, but I don't want to talk to him. I've detached, and as far as I'm concerned, there's nothing more to say."

"Shannon, you know I care a lot about you, but if you two still have unfinished business, I won't stand in the way."

He's such a gentleman. "Nope. No unfinished business. He made his choices, and I'm living my life. If he has anything else to say he can put it in a letter."

"Well, please know I would never pressure you, but I hope we can continue to see each other."

"I'm counting on it. I care about you as well, Max."

He drew her close, his eyes on hers. He reached out a finger and traced her cheek, then tucked a stray blond hair behind her ear. She tilted her face upward and let her eyes drift closed as he leaned in for their first real kiss. When she opened them again, she wasn't sure if she was seeing stars shine or just the moon, but his blue eyes beckoned, and she kissed him back.

They walked quietly to the car, arm in arm, enjoying each other. He opened her door, then took her in his arms once more.

"You're beautiful, you know that?" he murmured. "Inside and out. I'm so thankful I met you, Shannon Enright."

Chapter Ten

*E*rin McCall, who worked in the advertising department at the *Loughton Valley Herald*, asked Max on Wednesday if she could speak with him at lunch. They met in the café across the street.

"Hey, Erin, what's up?"

Erin leaned in and spoke quietly. "This is a little awkward, but I wanted to mention something and get your take on it. My cousin lives in Paden, a little town about thirty minutes from here. Well, anyway, Taylor visited me last weekend, and I took her to the Amaryllis for tea. We saw Rose when we walked in, and Taylor knew her—but she's never been to Loughton Valley before. They chatted for a few minutes at the register. Rose seemed super uncomfortable. I've never seen her like that before. Then Taylor said she'd see her next Wednesday, and we went to the tearoom.

"I asked her how she knew Rose, and she told me the strangest thing. Taylor works at the post office in Paden, and she said Rose comes in every Wednesday afternoon to pick up her mail from a post office box. Then she takes the mail to her car and reads it. Taylor said she can see the car from the window, and sometimes it looks like Rose is crying.

"Anyway, after a while, she comes back in the post office, puts the mail she got in the trash, and mails out one or two new things. Don't you think it's strange that Rose has a post office box in another town? I know you're interviewing her for the upcoming article—did she ever mention anything about Paden?"

"No. Maybe she's a secret agent." He grinned.

"Very funny. I was afraid you'd think I was exaggerating. Oh well, I just thought it was odd."

"There's probably a simple answer." Max shrugged. "Rose is one of Loughton Valley's most upstanding citizens. If she prefers to get some mail in another town, she must have a good reason."

"Yeah . . . I feel silly for mentioning it now. But it did seem odd she'd drive that far to get mail the same day every week, when she also has mail delivered daily at the shop and cottage. Guess I've been reading too many mysteries."

They finished their lunch and returned to the office. At his desk, Max opened his computer and began a Google search for *Rose Daniels.* Nothing. White Pages only listed her current address at the cottage, no previous addresses. He recalled how she had avoided questions about her family and her past in their interviews. She'd always changed the subject. He'd thought she was simply being humble and modest, wanting him to focus on the shop and her employees and volunteers, not her. He thought things over for a few minutes, then walked over to Jeremy's office in the research department.

"You busy, Jer?"

"Heck no. It's slow here today. What's up?"

"Could you do a little bit of digging for me? I'm interviewing Rose Daniels, owner of the Amaryllis in town. I'd like to know a bit more about her past so I can ask the right questions the next time

I interview her. She was busy, didn't really have time to answer all my questions. Might save a little time if I have more info before I meet with her next week."

"No problem, bro. That's a quick search. I'll email you what I find."

"Thanks."

Max returned to his desk, now remembering how firm Rose had been about not wanting her picture taken for the article. Coupled with Erin's information about the Paden post office box, Rose's evasion was beginning to look a bit suspicious. His phone dinged, announcing a new email. He opened it on his computer.

"Checked my usual sites; couldn't find a thing on your lady. Several Rose Daniels popped up, but they were all too young. Our Rose doesn't appear to exist before she moved to Loughton Valley. What's up with that?"

What indeed, Max wondered. He thought for a moment, then picked up his phone. Time to call in a favor with an old friend.

"Hey, Tracy. It's Max. How's it going?"

"About the same. Great to hear from you. Have you decided to come back to a real paper?"

"Nah. You know I got tired of the politics there. I love my little newspaper."

"What's up?"

"I'm wondering if you could do a little P.I. work for me."

"Like check the background on a girlfriend?" He laughed.

"Not hardly. I wrote an article on some local shop owners, and there are some unanswered questions about one lady. Her name is Rose Daniels in Loughton Valley. Could you check her out? You're the best investigator I know so if anyone can find this lady, it would be you."

"Happy to help. I'll get back to you. Take it easy, buddy."

"Thanks. I owe you." He had a twinge of guilt for checking up on Rose, but his curiosity outweighed the guilt.

Friday night on their dinner date, Max told Shannon what Erin had told him and the dead-end search he'd done on the internet. He didn't mention calling Tracy. "It could be nothing," he mused, "but on the surface, it looks like Rose might have a past she doesn't want revealed."

Shannon bristled. "What are you saying? You know Rose. She's the most honest person I know, utterly transparent. I can't believe you're thinking that."

"Well, being in the newspaper business might have jaded me a bit. It is strange though, Shannon. You can't argue with that."

"You know what? Let's drop the subject. I don't want to be talking about Rose behind her back."

"Yes, ma'am. How's your dinner?"

Chapter Eleven

Andrew's surprise visit continued to bother Shannon all week, so on Saturday evening, she called Claire and asked if she could think of any reason why Andrew had shown up and whether he had contacted Mark recently. Claire was as surprised and bewildered as Shannon was.

"Mark hasn't mentioned anything about Andrew for quite a while. He wouldn't have told him where you are, but it's probably not that hard to find out. Do you think he'll try to contact you again?"

"I have no idea. This is so confusing. Part of me wants to hear him out, but the other part wants to keep that door permanently closed. I don't want to get hurt again or be living with his drama."

"Yeah, it's a tough decision. You'll have to do what's right for you, Shannon. Hopefully, he won't bother you again since you made it clear you didn't want to talk to him."

"I tried to be clear, but he wasn't listening. He was pressuring me to talk to him, like he was entitled to be heard."

"Well, since you haven't heard from him in a week, that's a good sign. Keep me posted."

"I will. Have a good weekend. Talk again soon."

Shannon ended the call and worked hard to enjoy the rest of the weekend. With conscious effort, she managed to keep from getting lost in thoughts of Andrew.

That ended when she got home from work on Monday, however. She put Willow on the leash and walked out to the mailbox. There was a letter from Andrew. Back in the apartment, she fixed a cup of tea and slowly opened the letter, fingers shaking.

Dear Shannon,

I'm sorry for not giving you notice that I was coming to see you or that I wanted to talk to you. I incorrectly thought it would be better if we talked in person, but I understand why you chose not to talk to me. I guess that was being insensitive toward your feelings and, again, I'm sorry.

If you do have it in your heart to meet with me to let me explain, that would be a gift. An undeserved gift but appreciated. I'm asking you, for the sake of all that we had together in the past—our love, happy memories, and future plans—to give me a chance to talk to you again. You truly are, and always have been, the love of my life and I selfishly and stupidly walked away from you. I will regret that for the rest of my days.

You're the best thing that ever happened to me. I don't deserve another chance, but I have to try. I love you, Shannon, truly love you with all my heart. I can't imagine life without you. I'll do anything to win you back. Please consider talking with me. Tell me when and where, and I'll be there."

Love—with all my heart,

Andrew

Rising from the recliner, Shannon opened the drapes and stood gazing out the slider toward the lake. With a deep breath and fighting tears, she prayed. "God, I need Your help, Your wisdom. Please help me. Amen." Returning to the recliner, she read the letter again, more slowly, looking for clues about his sincerity—or lack of it.

How can I believe him after everything that he's done? Why would I want to open this Pandora's box? Why? She decided she didn't want to think about it anymore tonight. She would be more clear-headed in the morning.

"No, how could you do this to me?" she called out in her sleep. Suddenly awakened, she sat up in bed recalling the bad dream— the awful night when Andrew left, the hurtful things he'd said. The night her world completely disintegrated. Everything that had taken place after that night—the humiliation of telling family and friends, dividing possessions, the divorce, leaving her home, moving, the night she'd wanted to die—it all tumbled through her head. None of that could be undone, swept away, or covered over because Andrew was *sorry*. She had a busy day ahead at work, so she made some chamomile tea and sipped it, still pondering. Sleep was a long way off.

In the morning, she stood before the bathroom mirror longer than normal, acknowledging the bags under her eyes. She felt tired, old, and ugly; like she'd lived twenty years in the past few months. Sadness turned to tears and tears to wailing. *Why, Lord? Why?*

With no appetite for breakfast, she showered, put on extra makeup, styled her hair, and left for work. She was thankful she had a project deadline on Friday that would keep her engaged throughout the week. She might even have to stay late a few nights.

Max called Wednesday afternoon. "You might not believe it,

but I'm pretty good at fixing Szechuan chicken—I've got an authentic recipe from a restaurant in LA's Chinatown. Can I make it for you Friday night?"

"That sounds amazing. What time?"

"Is five thirty too early?"

"No. I've been working late every night, so by Friday, I'll be ready to leave early. What can I bring?"

"Not a thing. We're all set. Don't work too hard—see you soon."

She spent the rest of the week anticipating. She hadn't been to his house yet, and she was curious to see how he lived. She wondered if he was neat and organized or a more stereotypical bachelor with thrown-together décor. He had taken her to his office once— that was a little messy with books and files scattered about, but he was working a big project then which would explain it. *We'll see.* Either way, nothing would change the feelings she had for him.

She wrapped things up at work and left at 4:00 so she'd have plenty of time for primping. It felt good to fuss about choosing the right outfit for their dates. They'd been together almost every Saturday and Sunday since their first date, with an occasional added coffee or dinner date midweek. They were attending church together now, too, which was taking their relationship to a deeper level. She was thrilled to find him knowledgeable about the Bible and spiritual truths.

Once she was dressed, she grabbed a pretty plate from the back of the cupboard and loaded it with cookies she'd baked the night before. Fifteen minutes later, she was pulling into his driveway.

He met her at the door with a smile and a kiss. He hung up her coat and took the cookies to the kitchen, then gave her a quick tour. She was impressed with how each room was decorated—he definitely fit into the neat and organized category. The furniture was masculine, a comfortable mixture of modern, antique, and gentle restoration.

She stopped to admire an old oak desk. He grinned. "I tried

my hand at refinishing with this," he said. "Didn't realize how time consuming it could be."

"Really? You did a great job. I've painted a few wooden pieces but never tackled an actual restoration. I love oak. This is a beautiful piece."

They ended the tour in the living room, where he went to the sliding doors on the outside wall. "This is my newest project," he pronounced. She followed him into a glass-enclosed sunroom, surprised to find it warm. When she mentioned that, he motioned toward the windows.

"A little insulation works wonders. I added some radiant heat and good windows, and the room retains its warmth for quite a while. It's really a four-season room now. I spend a lot of time here, reading and listening to music. It's my peaceful place. I'll turn on the heat, and we'll have dessert out here. Well, enough about the house. Are you hungry?"

"Mmm, you bet. It smells delicious." He led her into the dining room, where she admired again his effort to make the evening special. He'd even set the table with fresh flowers and candles. Every evening with him was special regardless of what they had planned. She loved how well they worked together in the kitchen—they'd cooked together several times at her place.

He handed her a long spoon to stir the cooked rice while he lit the flame under the wok. "Everything's ready, I just need to reheat it a bit. There, all set." He pulled out a chair for her and pressed a quick kiss on her cheek.

She gave him a hug in return. "Thank you for inviting me— this looks wonderful."

"I apologize for not inviting you over sooner. I don't have a large repertoire of recipes, but the Szechuan hasn't let me down yet. I hope you like it." He held her hand and spoke the blessing.

She savored her first few bites. "*Mmm.* Honestly, this is some of the best chicken I've ever had. I'm impressed—and just the right amount of kick to it."

After dinner, they carried dessert into the sunroom. The full moon was high in the sky. Shannon couldn't help but marvel over it.

Max was happy to admire it with her. "And," he said, "because it's all conservation land back here, there's nothing to obstruct the view." He pointed to a small telescope set up in one corner. "Since I finished the room, I've become a stargazer—been reading up on the constellations too. Did you know scientists say there are ten times more stars in the night sky than grains of sand in *all* the deserts and beaches in the world? I can't wrap my head around that. God is awesome."

"Wow, that's almost unbelievable. I've lived in bigger cities most of my life. It wasn't always easy to see the stars. Kinda sad when you think about it. Here, it's wide open."

"It's one thing I love about living in a small town," Max said. He brought the telescope over in front of the sofa, adjusted it, and focused it toward the darkened sky. "Here, take a look." Leaning close, he showed her how to adjust the lens.

It took her a minute to get used to the apparatus, but when she did, she sucked in a breath and held it in surprise. "That's incredible. I can't believe what I've been missing." She moved the telescope slowly to take in more of the sky, then pulled away and rested her head on his shoulder. She sat quietly in the serenity of the moment, wishing time could stand still. He rested his head against hers, and she wondered if he was wishing the same thing.

He turned toward her, his eyes glistening in the moonlight. "Shannon, I'm falling in love with you. I love every minute I spend with you. I think about you all the time when we're apart. I haven't asked you about Andrew since Bridgeport because I wanted to give you time to sort things out. I want the best for you, but . . ." He made a silly half-smile and pulled away slightly. "Well . . . I think that would be me. But if you need space, I'll understand."

Those eyes get me every time. Wait. He loves me? Shannon swallowed hard. She was silent for a minute, then spoke hesitantly.

"I don't know what my reality is right now, Max. I haven't talked about it because I'm so confused. I love our time together too, and I want to continue our relationship. But I think I need to hear Andrew out, face-to-face, before I commit to anything with you. I'm not looking forward to it, but I think it's the right thing to do. I appreciate your trust. I guess the sooner I talk to him, the better it'll be. I was thinking about asking him to meet me for lunch next weekend. Probably some place halfway."

"I understand. Or at least I'm trying to." He shifted so he could see her better. "I thought about it the other day and wondered what I would do if I were in your shoes, if my ex contacted me. I don't know—I guess I would give her a chance to explain things." He took her hand. "I could be selfish and ask you not to bother with him, but I won't. I want you to be happy, and if that means . . . Andrew . . . well . . ."

He's making it harder. She wanted to tell Max she was falling for him too, but she couldn't, in good faith, commit until she talked to Andrew. She knew how much it hurt to be deceived by someone you love, and she was determined to be open and truthful with Max.

She squeezed his hand and, with a rueful smile, said, "Thanks, Max. You've been a gentleman since day one. I wish I weren't in this situation, but I am, so I have to face it. I'm grateful you believe in me enough to do what's right—even when it seems so wrong. I wish I could tell you something different right now, but I can't."

"It's okay. You're worth waiting for. Just don't keep me in the dark too long." He growled playfully.

She nodded and settled back in his arms.

Chapter Twelve

Snuggled in her recliner and nervously twirling her pen around in her hand, Shannon wondered if she could really trust her own judgment and feelings. So many unknowns and more questions than answers. Well, she'd just have to dive in head-first, based on what her gut was telling her.

Buoyed by a strong desire to do the right thing, but unsure what it was, she reread Andrew's letter and jotted down thoughts next to some of his statements.

"So . . . he's sorry? Such a shallow little word, like brushing crumbs off the table and making everything neat and tidy again. Hmph." She circled the "sorrys," then crossed each one out. "You know what you can do with your sorrys."

She read the next paragraph aloud, pausing intentionally to circle each "love."

"Ugh. Willow, he used the word 'love' five times. It's just a word, coming from him—it means nothing now. You know more about showing love than he does."

Her mind flashed back to their wedding day and their vows. Everyone had remarked about how much in love they were. *The happiest day of my life.* She snorted at the thought.

"Yours is a perfect love," Mark, their best man had said at the rehearsal dinner.

And Dad—"Always remember, Shannon, your love will carry you through the tough days." He'd whispered it to her right before he'd walked her down the aisle. Why did he say that, then, on that day? Was he thinking of normal tough days, or had he been questioning her decision to marry Andrew. *I'm doubting everything now.*

"He loves me with 'all his heart.'" Sarcasm dripped from her voice. Willow bumped her with her nose, but Shannon didn't notice. "If that was true, there wouldn't be another woman—or a baby—in your life," she shouted. "How am I supposed to respond to this?"

She crumpled the letter even as her mind flooded with vivid images of their honeymoon, decorating their first apartment, making plans to build their home, moving in . . .

"You ruined my life, Andrew Paul Enright! What are you doing now? And why?"

She looked at the wadded-up paper on the table in front of her. Part of her wanted to tear it up and forget she'd ever seen it—and him. The other part nudged her to give him a chance, to let him speak, face-to-face. Did she owe him that much?

Owe it or not, she needed to see his emotions, not just read the words. With jerky motions, she straightened the letter, folded it, and put it back into the envelope it had come in. Then she stuck it inside the book she was reading.

She pulled out her phone and googled locations. Finally, she typed a brief text: *Andrew, I will meet you next Sunday afternoon at 2:00 at Starbucks, 97 Winding Pond Road in Shelton, CT. Shannon.*

Nothing more she wanted to say. And meeting in a public place a decent distance from Loughton Valley seemed like the best option.

"There, done."

Anxious feelings crept in during the week, mostly in the lonely evenings after work. Max had sent a few short, sweet text messages saying he was thinking of her. They had warmed her heart, but they weren't much help in her dilemma. Friday night she called Claire.

"Hey, I sent Andrew a text saying I would meet him Sunday afternoon. At a Starbucks about forty-five minutes away."

"Big step, Shan. I hope it goes well for you. Good idea to meet where you can make a quick exit if you need to." She chuckled. "Better than a restaurant. What time on Sunday?"

"Two o'clock. I'll wait exactly fifteen minutes. If he's late, I'll leave. Punctuality never was his strong suit."

"Oh, yeah. I know how frustrated you used to get when he caused you to be late on our double dates. Which, now that I think about it, was quite a few times."

"Yep. Well, this time he better get his act together. There won't be a second chance if he misses this one."

"Good for you. Set those boundaries."

"I'm not letting Mom and Dad know anything about him contacting me. I don't think that would go over very well."

"I expect not. But you have to do what's right for you, and then you can explain things when it's the best time. Then again, there might not be anything to tell, depending how it goes on Sunday."

"True. The fewer people who know the better. I'll give you a call after the meeting . . . if it happens."

"Okay, talk to you then. I'm hoping it goes well, for your sake, you know."

❦

Early Sunday morning, she took a long run around the lake without Willow to burn off extra stress and energy. She ate a quick lunch, then went to choose an outfit. Her stomach was in knots as she fussed about what to wear until she realized how ridiculous that was. She wasn't trying to impress him—far from it. Putting on her favorite well-worn jeans and a bright red tee made her feel a bit empowered. *Nothing special, who cares what he thinks?*

Arriving at Starbucks a few minutes early, she chose a small table in the corner between two windows and sat down to wait. At two o'clock sharp, he walked in and spotted her at the table. He was wearing the shirt she'd given him for his birthday. *Nice try, buddy. Won't work.*

"Hi, Shannon," he said cheerfully. "You look wonderful. Thank you for agreeing to meet me. Can I get you a coffee—do you still like the coconut-mocha?"

"Plain black, thank you," she bristled.

She watched him walk away to place the order and thought he had lost weight. He looked good though, too good. His smile as he returned almost made her forget how much she resented him, so she quickly looked down at the table to avoid longer eye contact.

"Thanks."

"Did you have lunch?"

"Yes, before I left."

"Okay." He took a slow sip of coffee, then set it down. "I've rehearsed in my mind what I want to say to you today, but nothing's sounding right. There's no way to express my feelings in words—I tried in the letter." His hand shook as he picked up his coffee again. "I'm nervous, as you can tell. What I hope you understand is . . . I'll do anything to restore our relationship. Anything. I know it would take time, but I'm asking for a chance. If there's any way we can have a fresh start and a future . . . That's all I'm hoping for."

Shannon remained quiet, except for the slight tapping of her foot on the floor which had a calming effect.

When she didn't respond, he continued. "Look—I messed up, royally. I know. The biggest mess-up a guy could make. I gave up a beautiful, wonderful, faithful woman . . . for . . . a fling. No way to sugarcoat it. That's what it was; it's what I did. And I regret it now more than you can imagine."

A fling? A fling that resulted in a baby! She looked straight into his eyes for the first time since he sat down. But she remained quiet. *There's a lot more he needs to say.*

"If you tell me you never want to see me again or hear from me, I'll be respectful and not contact you. You have every right to feel that way. I don't deserve you or a second chance with you. You were the best thing that ever happened to me. I can't explain why I've been so stupid and caused you so much pain—" He stopped talking as a tear seeped out the corner of one eye. "Excuse me, I'll be right back."

Shannon had been prepared to experience a range of feelings— confusion, nervousness, sadness, anger . . . But she wasn't prepared to deal with the strange feeling of hope that was tickling the back of her throat. In her heart, she hoped he was sincere—that he did love her and want her. But in her mind, she was guarded. She had to be.

He returned, composed, and smiled slightly.

She sat up a little straighter, crossed her legs, and mustered courage to speak. "I'll be honest. I don't know what I'm feeling. This is all very sudden. Obviously, it was a shock seeing you in the parking lot. So much has happened since you left. I know about Lela . . . and Sienna." She reached into her purse for a tissue and dabbed her eyes.

"I know you do. Mark told me."

"I know you fathered a child while you were married to me. I can't describe to you how painful all this has been. And still is. But you're a father. You have the responsibility of a child now. I don't know what to do with that."

Andrew shifted nervously when she said "father." He cleared his throat, pushed the coffee cup to the side, and looked down at the table. "I can't expect you to accept this, at least not now."

"Not ever."

"I've tried to put myself in your shoes many times over the last few weeks. I don't know how I would handle it either. I'm only asking for a chance to restore our relationship because what we once had was beautiful. I was selfish and stupid—I didn't realize that everything I needed, I already had with you. I'm sorry."

"I need time to think about all this. I really don't want to talk about it anymore now."

"Of course. I just didn't want to wait any longer to tell you how I'm feeling—about you and our life together."

She shrugged into her coat, ready to leave. He leaped to his feet in an attempt to pull out her chair for her, but she resisted and moved it herself. "I have your number." She knew her cheeks were flushed, and she felt like she was shaking inside.

"Okay. I won't contact you unless I hear from you, but I do hope I will hear something good, even if it takes a while. May I walk you to your car?"

"I'd prefer you don't."

"All right. But I hope you know how much I appreciate the chance to see you and talk to you. I've missed you more than you can imagine, Shannon. I'm a complete mess without you in my life." He made an awkward step toward her.

Her hand shot up, and she shifted sideways. "Goodbye."

"Goodbye. And thank you."

She held it together until she was in the car, then the tears flowed. She checked her rearview mirror to be sure he hadn't followed her. He was walking in the other direction, so she pulled out of the parking lot and into the next road. It led through a housing development and out to a plaza. She pulled into a parking spot, turned up the radio, and let her confusion and frustration out.

"I hate him! I really do." she wailed. It took a few minutes, but eventually she was composed enough to continue the drive home.

She went straight to Willow's crate, leash in hand. "Let's go out, girl," she said. The dog's energy was a good distraction as they tumbled out the door, but her worries soon took over. Her mind raced as they walked, recalling the words he had spoken, his mannerisms, expressions, his smile. *Darn, I wish he didn't look so good.*

Back in the house, she heated a can of soup and made a cup of tea, then called Claire.

"Hey, Claire. My emotions are all over the place."

"So what'd he say?"

"Not much more than what was in the letter. He wants to . . . quote: 'restore our relationship.' Whatever that means. And he said he 'messed up and had a fling,' well, hello! That's not a newsflash."

"How'd you end the conversation?"

"I told him I had his number. He can interpret it anyway he wants. He asked to walk me to my car, but that wasn't going to happen." She rose from her chair and paced around the living room. "Now I'm wondering what's wrong with me, because part of me wants him back and I don't know why."

"Because you loved him, silly," Claire interrupted. "You were bonded to him for all those years. Part of you probably still loves him. The only reason it hurts so much is because you loved him so much."

"I guess, but it would be a lot easier if I could just hate him. I thought I had completely detached after I found out about the baby. This is so complicated, Claire. Impossibly complicated."

"It must feel impossible, but you have time to sort things out for yourself before you talk to him again—if you do. You'll figure this out. You're smart and level-headed, Shan; always have been. And I know you pray, so God will give you the answers you need. Just be sure to take care of yourself, promise?"

She wondered if Claire was worried she might try to harm herself again. "I promise."

Chapter Thirteen 🌹

Wednesday evening, Rose greeted Max at the shop and walked with him to the Tea Cozy area. "Please help yourself to a beverage and some pastries."

"Thanks." He filled a cup and snack plate and sat at a table. Rose finished straightening up a few centerpieces on the tables, then joined him at his.

"Thanks for meeting with me again, Rose," he began. "I know you're a busy lady. I have the rough copy of the article for you to look over." He handed her a few pages and waited as she read through the text.

"Oh, my! This is so nice. But you make it sound like I have a big shop." She grinned.

"Not big in size, but big in importance in our town. I also interviewed some of your customers, and everything in the article is true. People really respect you. And most come in here for more than just a bouquet or a pastry. There's vibrancy in this shop—and it's because of you."

"That's so kind of you to say, Max. It's the Lord's work—He sends the ones here who need a little kindness and hope. It's what I try to offer, the Lord's kindness and hope. We all need it, don't we?"

"Yes, we certainly do. Is there anything you'd like me to change in the article? Did I leave out anything?"

Rose scanned the article again. "No, what you wrote is wonderful. Thank you."

"Oh, and that reminds me . . . I thought I would include a sentence or two about your life before the Amaryllis. Anything you would like to include in that area?" He watched carefully for her reaction.

She stood up, bustled over to the counter, and filled another plate with pastries and brought a bag to the table. When she came back, she waved her hand airily. "Oh, Max, there's nothing exciting to report about me. Let's just focus on the Amaryllis. I'm sure it's the only thing local people would be interested in reading about. Here, take some pastries home with you for breakfast tomorrow."

"Thank you. I'll enjoy them. And one more thing . . . have you changed your mind about being in the photo? It's just logical you should be in the pic—you *are* the shop."

"Now, now . . . people don't want to see an old lady in the newspaper. I thought about it again, and I really would like Shannon to be in the photo. She's so photogenic with her contagious smile, and all the customers love her. And I think there's one in particular who is very fond of her." She tapped his shoulder.

"I can't argue with that. Shannon it is. I'll set it up with her and then we can work out a time with you. Think about where in the shop you'd like the shoot and if we need to stage anything."

"Oh, I've been thinking about that. I'd like one shot at the counter with the amaryllis plants in the background, maybe one in front of the shop door, and another in the Tea Cozy area with some customers. But I'll defer to your professional judgment. All your photographs in the paper are top-notch."

"Thanks. I'll reach out to Shannon and get back to you as soon as I can. Have a wonderful night, Rose," he said as he started to leave.

"And you also, my dear. See you again soon. Oh . . . don't forget the pastries."

"Oops. I would be kicking myself in the morning for sure. Thanks again. Good night."

She's definitely hiding something. I need to find out what it is.

Saturday morning, Shannon's cell rang. She turned off the stove and moved the frying pan to a cool burner. Her heart fluttered when she saw who it was. "Hi, Max. Nice to hear from you."

"Hey, Shannon. Been thinking about you, but this is more of a business call, you might say. I met with Rose again, and she insists you should be in the photo for the newspaper article. Just wondering how you feel about it?"

"You couldn't convince her, huh?"

"No, I couldn't argue with her when she said you are photogenic and have a 'contagious smile.' Describes you perfectly."

"Ahh, she's so sweet. I'd be honored to represent her in the photo. What do you have in mind?"

"She mentioned a couple of ideas, so I'm wondering when you would be free. Shouldn't take long, and I would love to see you again."

"I'm volunteering this afternoon from one to three. Would it work then?"

"Works perfectly. I'll let Rose know. See you soon."

It's so good to hear his voice. I've missed him. She reheated the pan, finished cooking the eggs, toasted the bread, and quickly ate. After a short walk with Willow, she did some light housework, paid some bills online, and began getting ready. She chose a black-and-white striped top and white slacks. She thought about how special Max always made her feel when they were together—their dates and memories at the apartment, long walks, cooking together, watching movies, playing Mahjong, which he had patiently taught her. Part of her wanted to just tell Andrew to buzz off so she could resume everything with Max. Everything seemed so perfect when they were together. He was trustworthy. How could she ever trust Andrew again? It would be easier to trust anyone other than him. Could their past be repaired?

❧

"Hi, Rose."

"Good afternoon, Shannon. Max is in the Tea Cozy. He has a few ideas for the photos—thanks for agreeing to do this. Take as long as you two need, it hasn't been too busy today."

"Okay, will do." She stored her purse behind the counter and joined Max.

He pulled out a chair for her at one of the thankfulness tables. "You look lovely, as always."

"Thank you. I have a few more sweaters in the car if you don't think this one will photograph well."

"It's a perfect choice." He squeezed her shoulder. "I've been thinking about you a lot. How are you holding up?"

"I met with him briefly last Sunday." She sighed. "I haven't committed to seeing him again. I still need time to sort things out."

"Did he treat you okay?"

"Yeah, he was nervous but nice. It was pretty awkward. I told him I would contact him and asked him not to contact me until then."

"Good. He should be accepting everything on your terms." He

smiled. "So, are you ready to talk about your big photoshoot?" After briefly describing Rose's ideas about shooting at the floral counter, out front, and in the Tea Cozy, he said, "I'll take several at each spot—distance and close-ups. Ready?"

They walked to the counter, where he gave her some hints about position, posture, head angle, and so forth. When he gently moved her shoulder and tilted her face to set up a pose, she looked into his eyes and couldn't help the tingle that raced along her nerves. *Stop that.* He took some more shots outside by the front door, at the counter filling a vase with fresh flowers, and ringing out a customer at the antique register. In the Tea Cozy, he captured her pouring tea and serving pastries to customers at a thankfulness table.

"You certainly are photogenic," he said, holding out his camera. "Here, take a look at these." They reviewed the photos with Rose and agreed upon two—one outside by the front door and one inside. "The article should go to press next week, so I'll email the proofs to both of you on Monday."

Turning to Rose, he asked, "Do you have any last-minute changes or additions to the article?"

"No. The photos of Shannon will be a wonderful addition."

"Okay, great. Watch for the email."

Shannon returned to the floral counter to help a customer. Max followed.

"I know I said I wouldn't pressure you," he said softly. "I'll keep my promise, but I really do miss you. Maybe we could have dinner sometime." His blue eyes conveyed his sincerity.

"I've missed you too. Dinner would be nice."

"Is tonight too soon, or do you have plans?"

"No plans."

"Great. Six o'clock okay?"

"Perfect; I'm looking forward to it."

His smile grew larger as he nodded, gathered his photography equipment, and left.

The article came out on Friday, and before Shannon even made it into the Amaryllis on Saturday, she'd heard the buzz. The place was crowded. In addition to the regulars in the Tea Cozy, there were first-time customers and other merchants in town who'd dropped in to congratulate Rose.

"Thanks again for coming in, Shannon," Rose breathed. Her eyes sparkled. "We would be short-handed without you today. It's as busy as Valentine's week!" She bustled back to the counter to wait on another new customer.

Shannon enjoyed answering questions about Rose's repaired containers. Some customers purchased bouquets, while others just wanted one of her artistic pieces for their homes. More than one customer was disappointed to learn the blue and gold kintsugi vase at the counter wasn't for sale. Throughout the afternoon, every table in the Tea Cozy was filled with customers. Libby and Shannon offered to stay until closing, and Rose accepted appreciatively. It was an exhausting but satisfying day.

Chapter Fourteen

Sunday after church, Shannon pulled out her journal. She hadn't written in it for a while, but doing so helped her think. And she needed to think.

She summarized the meeting with Andrew, then added some thoughts about what he'd said and her feelings about it. Turning the page, she began jotting down her thoughts about time she'd spent with Max. Finally, she leaned back in the recliner and read everything out loud. The contrasts were stunning. Confusion versus clarity. Sadness versus happiness. Suspicion versus trust. Coldness versus warmth. Distance versus attention . . .

She slammed the book shut. "Why am I struggling about what to do?" The words burst from her lips, frustration obvious. "Anyone can see it—it's so clear! . . . Except it isn't, not really." No, it was clear as mud.

Well, whatever it was, she was tired of the confusion. The best thing to do was to see Andrew again, give him a chance, and give herself the opportunity to discern his true motives, if possible. She didn't want to regret not having closure.

She thought another moment, then grabbed her phone and typed out a text. *Andrew, I believe we have more to discuss. There's an Olive Garden in Shelton. Would you be able to meet me there for lunch next Sunday at one o'clock? Please text a reply, no calls.* As soon as she hit Send, she questioned herself. *I hope this isn't a mistake. How long will Max wait for me to make a decision?*

❦

"How many in your party?" the Olive Garden hostess asked.

"Two, but the other person isn't here yet." Andrew looked around the crowded dining room. "Could we have a private table, please?"

"Sure, we have a few open tables in the back room, if it's okay."

"That would be perfect, thank you. I'll wait for her here." All around him, couples faced each other at cozy tables, talking, laughing, smiling. *This will be us soon. Shannon will come around. She has to.*

When Shannon arrived five minutes later, he greeted her with a smile. "Surprise. I got here early this time. Can you believe it?"

She gave him a half-smile but didn't say anything. That was fine. He turned to the hostess. "We're ready to be seated," he said politely.

The hostess led them to the back room, placed menus on the table and introduced their server. Andrew didn't wait.

"Would you like an appetizer," he asked. "I know how much you love shrimp cocktails." He reached across the table and opened her menu to the appetizer page.

She raised an eyebrow and closed the menu. "No, thank you. Let's just order. I would like the chicken margherita, please."

"And for you, sir?"

"I'll have the salmon, thank you."

Once the server had collected the menus and filled their water glasses, Andrew leaned in toward Shannon. He let his gaze sweep over her face. She wasn't as easy to read as she used to be. "You look lovely, Shannon. I've been checking my phone every day for a text from you. I even checked the mailbox." He laughed. "Thank you for meeting me."

She unfolded the napkin and placed it on her lap. "I know you're trying to make this not so awkward, but the reality is, it's still very uncomfortable. Let me make this clear to you—we aren't a couple. This isn't a date either. I don't want you to get the wrong idea. It's just some time to talk about a few things. Nothing more."

He leaned back in his chair. She wasn't going to make this easy. No problem. He knew what he was doing. "Okay, I can respect that. I'm sorry I've made things uncomfortable. Is there anything I can do or say to make you feel more comfortable now?"

"Just be honest, Andrew. No games, no expectations. I need you to be honest."

"I am. My life's an open book now. You know everything—everything! The good, the bad, and the ugly." He sighed. "Of course, you probably question if there's anything good anymore. I hope you'll think about all the good we had—most of our marriage was good, wasn't it?"

"I don't know." Her voice was flat. "I question everything now. What I thought was good got lost in the recent ugly. I don't know what was real anymore."

"I'll do anything to show you how much I want a future with you. I'll go to counseling. Anything."

"You said some awful things before you left—like I was worthless and you deserved to be happy, but couldn't be with me—and that's only a few."

"Aw, Shannon. I wasn't myself in those last months. I lost my way. I hope you know, Lela pursued me; I didn't go looking for an affair. I guess you could say, I got caught in her web. That's a good way to describe it."

"Oh! So let me get this straight. It's not your fault because you were 'pursued'?" She set her fork down abruptly and looked straight into his eyes, waiting for a response.

Oops. "What I mean is, she tricked me." He felt his face turning red. "I guess I didn't say it right. She was persuasive, very persuasive. I lost sight of what was really important in my life—you and our future together."

She shook her head. "There is such a disconnect in what you're saying. If I was important to you, then why did you throw it all away? Didn't it ever occur to you that maybe somebody might flirt with me while we were married? Or hint at something more? They did, but I never considered it—I never would. We were *married.* That's the difference between us."

"I know, I know. I'm an idiot. I blew it. Big time. The worst thing a husband could do. You're the better person, Shannon, you always have been. And you were faithful. I don't deserve you, but if you'll give me a chance, I'll make it all up to you."

She fussed with the food on her plate, pushing it back and forth with her fork. "That's a big chance, Andrew. For even more hurt in the end. I don't know you anymore. Did I ever know the *real* you?"

"Look—I'll quit my job and move to Connecticut. I'll do anything you ask me to do. Nothing matters to me, Shannon, except you. Please?"

"Why? What's so urgent?" She shook her head again. "I don't know if I can ever trust you again. You destroyed my trust, and I don't know how to get it back. I don't know if I can trust *anyone* after what you've done."

"What do you mean? Who? Are you dating someone else?"

Her eyes sparked fire. "That is none of your business. We're divorced—we have separate lives."

"Fair enough. I shouldn't have asked." He paused, then gave her the grin he knew she couldn't resist. "I just wanted to know if I have competition. I'm sure there are a lot of guys who are interested in you—and why wouldn't they be."

"Don't be flip!"

"I'm sorry. Can I ask, do I have a chance—if we take things slow? Do you ever think about the wonderful years? All the good things we did together?"

"Yeah, I did. At first. But the memories became less wonderful and more painful. Our whole past was all a lie."

"No, it wasn't. That's what I'm trying to say, Shan. It was real, very real. And we can have it all again. Maybe even better. I don't deserve it, but what I'm hoping for is—your forgiveness. Other couples have survived what we've gone through."

She blew out a frustrated breath. "No, Andrew. That's just it—it's not what *we've* gone through. It's what *I've* gone through. You don't understand. You left. You started a new life with someone else, brought a child into the world—" She stopped and crossed her arms. "And you know what? We have to talk about the baby. What's your plan? How much are you involved in her life?"

"Ahh, I'm still figuring that out." He moved his water glass and rearranged the extra napkins on the table. "We can talk about it later. Right now we need to focus on *us*. If we get us straightened out, everything else will fall into place."

"No, this is an important issue. How often do you see her? You aren't living with Lela, so what's your custody situation? I assume you're paying child support."

"Everything's pretty loose right now, nothing's official. I see her on weekends and usually take her to my parents' house. We're all still getting used to having a baby around. And if *we* were together—"

"She's not ours." Shannon's face was hard. "I don't know. I just don't know if I could do what you're asking. Things can't be undone. And I'm not sure I want to live in your reality."

"But don't you remember what Pastor Clarkson used to say about forgiveness? Forgiveness means letting go of the pain, remember?"

For a moment, she froze. Then she carefully placed her fork on the table. "I don't need a lecture from you about forgiveness. Or about pain! You have no idea what I've been through—the shame, humiliation, rejection. It's been horrible. And I can't just say, 'okay, let's start over.'" She picked up her purse to leave.

"No. Shannon, don't go." He made his voice calm, even. "I'm saying all the wrong things. I hope you can see through the words—I want to try to have what we once had. I need you in my life, Shan. You've always been the best part of my life."

She placed her purse back on the chair but pushed her plate away. "I want to believe you. But it'll take time—maybe a long time before I trust you again."

"That's all I'm asking for—time. I don't care how long it takes. I'm going to prove my love to you. I want to make a new commitment to you—this time forever. I've had a huge wake-up call; I see things clearly now." He reached across the table and touched her hand. "I know without any hesitation I want to spend the rest of my life with you."

When she didn't pull away, he tapped the top of her hand, then gently curled his fingers around hers and squeezed. "You're the only one I want to be with."

Slowly, she pulled her hand back and placed it on her lap. "I'm trying. All I can say is I'll try."

"I promise I'll make everything up to you. You'll see. Everything will be better than it ever was before. Can I see you a couple times a week? I'll come to Connecticut, just say the word. I don't care about the drive—I'll come anytime."

"Let's take it one week at a time. Sunday afternoons are good. I have a commitment on Saturdays—I volunteer at a local shop."

"It's just like you to volunteer; you're the greatest. Let me know where and when to meet you. Hey, is there an ice-skating rink in your town? Do you still skate? I know how much you loved it."

"There's one about twenty minutes away from my apartment. I've been a couple times. I'll send you the address. What about two o'clock?"

The server left the bill, and Andrew laid some cash on the table.

"It's a date. Or . . . should I not say that?" He winked as he stood up.

She smiled back. "It's a trial date."

"Can I give you a hug?"

She nodded. He held her tightly for a few moments, then she pulled away.

"Is it okay if I call you once in a while?"

She shook her head. "Let's talk next Sunday."

"Okay. I'll walk you to your car."

A smile stretched across his face as Andrew watched her drive away. Overall, that had been a successful afternoon.

We're on our way now. Exactly like I planned.

Shannon was distracted as she drove home. Her emotions were all over the place. "I'm so confused," she said aloud. "Why did I let him hug me? And . . . why did it feel so good?"

She decided to call Claire, but when she did, Mark answered the phone.

"Hi, Shannon, it's Mark. We were going to call you tonight. Claire told me you were meeting with Andrew. Umm . . . I'm sorry, but she can't talk right now. We're at the hospital . . . she's having a procedure. We lost the baby."

"Oh, I know, she told m—wait. *What?* Oh, Mark. I'm so sorry. I didn't know she was pregnant again."

"Yeah, we didn't tell anyone this time. It's easier this way. She's doing okay; she's a trooper. She tries not to let me know how disappointed she is, but it's written all over her face. It's another loss—we were hoping and praying this time would be different."

"I can't imagine how painful this is—for both of you. Please tell her I love her and to take care of herself. Tell her I'll call in a day or two?"

"I'll tell her. Goodbye."

Shannon disconnected the call, her hands shaking. She turned her heart heavenward. "Oh, God, that's not fair. Please help Claire heal from another painful loss."

🌸

Things had slowed down to normal on Saturday at the Amaryllis. "Good morning, Rose."

"Well, good morning to you, Shannon," Rose replied, peering over three bouquets on the counter ready to be picked up.

"Where do you need me today?"

"I got a new shipment of flowers yesterday. Inventory got pretty low after last weekend—I'm not complaining, you know. Would you mind straightening up the cooler and organizing the flowers?"

"Sure thing." She grabbed her jacket and started straightening the flower bins.

Libby popped her head in the cooler doorway. "Hey, Shannon, could I talk with you after your shift is over? If you don't have plans?"

"No plans. Do you want to meet in the Tea Cozy?"

"No, I'd rather go to the coffee shop down the street. Give me a shout when you're ready to go."

"Okay, probably around eleven. See you then." *I wonder what's on her mind. And why she doesn't want to talk here. I hope everything's okay—she seems agitated and she's been through a lot.*

Rose pushed the door open with her hip and peered in. She was holding the large punchbowl in both arms. "The cooler looks great," she said brightly. "Thank you. Would you mind working the counter next? I'm behind on repairing containers, so I'll be in the back for a while."

Shannon assured her that would be fine, and Rose scurried off, the broken pieces inside the bowl clanging as she went.

At eleven o'clock, Rose came to the front, and Libby and Shannon headed out to the coffee shop together. Inside, Libby looked around quickly.

"Good, no one I know in here." Shannon looked at her quizzically as they got their coffees and sat down.

"What's up, Lib? Is everything okay?"

"I don't know. I need to talk to someone about something I discovered. I know I can trust you."

"What is it?"

Libby sighed and swirled the steaming liquid in her cup. "Monday morning, Rose asked me to straighten up her cottage. She's been so busy in the shop since the article came out, she hasn't had time to keep her place tidy and dusted. I'm happy to help wherever she needs me, so I started dusting the living room. You know that photo in the wooden frame on top of her rolltop desk—the one of her with her four grandkids?"

"Yeah, she seems really proud of that photo."

"Well, I accidentally knocked it down. I guess I was rushing too much. When it hit the floor, the glass broke. I picked it up, and the frame was loose too. I was trying to put it back together, when I noticed there was another photo behind the one she had displayed. I had to take everything out to reposition it. The second photo was a picture of Rose and four young kids. She looked younger; her hair was short and styled, she had on a beautiful dress. Oh, and she was wearing her pin, but it wasn't damaged. And there was writing on the photo: 'To Grandma Ruth, Love from Sam, Noah, Ava, and Caitlyn.'"

"All different names than her grandkids?"

"Yes, and those four kids weren't the ones in the other photo, either. I put everything back together and told Rose I'd replace the glass, but . . . Shannon . . . she had such a strange look when I told her about it. Like, she was really nervous. Then she told me not to worry about it, that she'd fix it, and she walked straight out to the cottage. She left so fast, I didn't mention that I'd seen the other photo."

"There's probably a simple explanation—maybe Ruth is a pet name the kids call her."

"Yeah, but those kids weren't the ones she has told us are her grandkids. And they had totally different names. You know how much I love her but . . . the look on her face was so strange. It felt like she was hiding something. She definitely didn't want me to fix the frame." She hesitated. "I'm a little ashamed to admit this, but yesterday while she was with a customer, I went back to the cottage and checked the frame. That other photo's gone."

Shannon propped her chin on her fist. "I don't know what to think of it, either, Libby. But we know Rose. I'm sure it's nothing to be concerned about."

"Mmm . . . you're probably right. Maybe I read too much into it. I feel better talking to you about it. Thanks." They finished their coffee and left the shop.

Shannon watched as Libby went back to the Amaryllis, then she walked to her car. *This is the second time someone has said Rose is hiding something. First Max and now Libby. What could she possibly be hiding?*

Andrew was waiting for Shannon at the Pavilion, the indoor ice-skating rink in Milford. He greeted her with a kiss on the cheek.

"It's good to see you kept your skates. I remember when we

bought them. You must have tried on ten pairs before you settled on those." He laughed. "And if I remember correctly, they were the most expensive."

"Yes, they were—because they were the best. And look how long they've lasted."

He reached for her hand to lead her onto the ice, then clasped it firmly as he matched his stride to hers. It had been a long time since they'd skated together. She had forgotten how nice it was. Tension visibly left her face as they glided around the rink, talking about old times, and occasionally laughing. She actually relaxed and followed his lead.

"Ready?" he asked mischievously.

"I think so." She grinned, and he twirled her like they had done a hundred times before. Turning around, he skated backward, looking into her eyes.

"Aw, Shannon. The world melts away when I'm with you. We make a good team, don't we?"

"We've always skated well together—we've had a lot of practice." They made several more loops around the rink.

"Ready for a break?"

"Sure." They got frappés, then found a bench where they could watch the other skaters.

"So, tell me about your job." He listened while Shannon gave him the highlights. He smiled at her approvingly. "I'm glad you found a job you like. I'm sure you're doing great there."

Conversation flowed easily, and time passed quickly. They sashayed around the rink a few more times until Shannon laughingly declared she couldn't go another lap.

He was happy to stop. "I worked up an appetite," he said. "Do you know a good restaurant around here?"

"I do, a great little diner. You can follow me."

After dinner he walked her to her car. "Shannon, today has been the best. Thank you. I had to pinch myself out there on the ice—it felt like old times. Did you feel it too?"

"It's a start. I still need to take things slow."

He moved closer and wrapped his arms around her. She didn't resist, so he bent his head and kissed her.

"Thank you for today. Thank you for being who you are—who you've always been. When can I see you again?"

She backed away, fumbling with her gloves. "There's a movie playing in Bridgeport I'd like to see. Next Sunday?"

"It's a date. And dinner before the movie?"

"Sure. I'll send you the details where to meet."

He opened her car door and thanked her again, then watched as she drove away. He was so dang irresistible.

After work the next day, Shannon decided it was time to tell her parents she was seeing Andrew. The phone call didn't go any better than she'd expected it to.

"Please try to understand, I think I should give him a chance. If things work out, then it's worth the risk I'm taking. And if they don't, then at least I know I tried. I can live with it."

"I don't trust him, honey." Dad responded. "Don't trust him at all. He's already revealed his true character and that's not likely to change. He doesn't look like he's missing you too terribly around town."

Shannon heard Mom shushing him in the background. She could picture Dad's shrug as he continued. "Anyway, you be careful. As far as I'm concerned, he doesn't deserve a second chance, not after what he's done. What about that nice guy at the newspaper you told us about? We thought you were dating him."

"Max—yes, we were dating, but we're taking a break for a while."

"Use discernment, Shannon. We don't want you to get hurt again."

"I know—thanks. I'll call again next weekend. I love you." *I can't expect them to understand; they're being protective. It'll take time for them to come around, but I hope they do.*

❦

Tuesday morning, Max was typing away at his computer in the office when his cell announced a call. "Hi, Tracy." It was his investigator friend.

"Got a minute?"

"Yeah, I'm ready for a break. I'd almost given up on you." He laughed. "What'd you find out?"

"Your lady is a mystery," Tracy said. "I've searched everything, but there's no trail for her before she moved to Loughton Valley. I'd suspect she's changed her name. Do you have an idea why? Or the state where the name change could have been filed?"

"Not a clue. She's really evasive about her past. Really? Nothing?" He scratched his head. "Well, thanks for the effort, anyway. I knew if anyone could track her down, it would be you."

"Sorry I couldn't help. Hey, don't be a stranger—come see us here sometime."

"I'll try to work it in—it would be great to see everyone. Thanks again."

Chapter Fifteen 🌹

Chili was simmering in the Crock-Pot. Rose took her cast iron skillet out of the oven and let the cornbread cool, finished setting the table for two, and checked the time. Pastor Dalton was due to arrive any moment with someone new who needed her help.

Right on time, there was a knock at the door. She answered it, and Pastor Dalton ushered a pregnant young woman into the house. He wasted no time making the introductions.

"Rose, this is Hadley."

"Hello, Hadley. I'm glad you came. Thank you, Pastor, for bringing her."

"Hadley, you're in good hands here. Call me if you need anything."

The girl nodded, her troubled eyes glancing nervously around the room. "Thank you," she murmured.

"You're welcome." Pastor Dalton placed her suitcase next to the kitchen table and left.

"May I take your jacket?" Rose asked. The girl struggled a bit, ungainly in her pregnancy, so Rose helped her get it off. Then she hung it on a nearby hall tree and turned with a smile.

"Have a seat, dear. I've made some chili and cornbread." She filled the bowls, cut the cornbread, and added a pat of butter to the plates. "What would you like to drink? I have coffee, tea, and ginger ale."

"Ginger ale, please. Thank you. You have a lovely home."

"Thank you. Pastor mentioned you live in an apartment on Marcus Road. That's not too far away. How long have you lived there?"

"Three years, with my boyfriend. It's a nice place."

"And are you working?"

"Yeah, I've been a teacher's aide at East Heights for two years now. I'm with the fourth graders this year."

"Good for you. That can be a tough job—I'm sure the kiddos love you."

"It's mutual. I love my job, even on the days when the kids don't cooperate. I feel like I make a difference, you know?"

After dinner, they moved to the living room for tea and home-made cookies. The girl had relaxed a bit, but as she glanced back toward the kitchen and caught sight of her suitcase, she tensed up again. "Did Pastor Dalton tell you about my problem?"

"He did, but . . . why don't you tell me, in your own words?"

She sighed deeply. "I think . . . I think I need . . . to get . . . an abortion." She paused for a sip of her tea. "Tom, my boyfriend, the father of my baby—he's not ready to get married or have a family. I was trying to be careful, but I guess I missed a pill. He doesn't want this baby. I told a friend at work, and she recommended I talk to Pastor Dalton before I make a final decision. He's really nice."

"Yes, he is. How do you feel about being pregnant? About the baby?"

Hadley touched her belly. "I love being pregnant . . . and I love my baby. I don't know what to do. Tom pretty much told me it's him or the baby." She bit her lip. "I really love him. We've been together for four years. We've talked about getting married and . . . I thought he just needed a little more time to make a commitment. When I found out I was pregnant, I wanted to get married right away, but he's really upset. He said he's leaving if I have the baby. He's pulled away from me—" She swallowed hard, her gaze focused on something outside the window.

"I just want things to be the way they were, you know? It's terrible timing."

"Oh, my dear," Rose crooned. "You are carrying a precious child of God. Every child is precious. What is your heart telling you?"

"I know it's wrong to have an abortion. But I don't want to lose Tom. And I can't support myself and raise a baby alone."

"Have you considered another option besides abortion?"

"You mean adoption? Pastor Dalton talked to me about it. He said he can put me in touch with someone who would help with the details."

"Yes." Rose nodded. "They would help you through every step." Hadley sniffed, and Rose observed the exhaustion in her slight frame. She stood. "Well, I'm sure you're tired. Let me show you to your room. We can talk more tomorrow. If you want to sleep in, I'll leave some pastries and juice in the kitchen. I have to open the shop at nine o'clock, but I'll check in on you. You can rest here."

She led the way upstairs, carrying Hadley's suitcase. "Here you go. There are blankets in the closet, and your bathroom is right next door. You make yourself at home."

"Now, can I pray for you before we say goodnight?"

Hadley looked surprised, but nodded. Taking her hands, Rose began to pray.

"Lord, guide this young girl and protect her baby. Thank you for bringing her here. Give her courage to make the right decision. Amen."

A fragile smile brightened the girl's face as Rose finished. "Thank you," she murmured. "Good night."

"Good night, dear. Sleep well."

🌹

Hadley wandered into the shop around nine thirty the next morning. Rose set the flowers she'd been working with on the counter and greeted her cheerily.

"Good morning, Hadley. Did you eat breakfast?"

"Yes, thank you. What a cute shop. I've driven past but never stopped in before. Do you mind if I look around a bit?"

"Please do. There's a small tea shop through the door." Rose returned to the counter where a customer stood waiting.

A young man appeared in the doorway, looked around, and rushed over to Hadley. "There you are."

"Tom?" Startled, she dropped the vase she'd been admiring. "Oh no! Look what happened. And why did you come here?"

"I told you not to do this," he said sternly. "You don't need anyone giving you any advice. This is our decision; no one else needs to be involved. Get your things and let's go."

Rose appeared with a broom and dustpan. Turning to the young man, she said, "Hello. My name is Rose. What's yours?" She extended a hand, but the gesture wasn't returned.

"I'm Tom. I've come to take her home."

"Hadley, do you want to leave?"

"No, I don't." Turning to Tom, she propped a hand on her hip. "I told you I would be here for a couple days and then I'll be home. You've embarrassed me, storming in here like this. Rose, I'm sorry about the vase. I'll pay you for it."

"Not to worry, dear—that vase was already broken." She began whisking up the pieces, keeping herself between the couple. Tom spoke louder.

"Well, you remember what I said. Don't let anyone get in your head. I'll expect you home in two days, no later." He scowled and walked out.

Hadley lowered her head toward Rose who was still sweeping the floor. "Here, let me finish cleaning up the mess I made."

"Almost done, dear. These old cement floors aren't very forgiving." She emptied the dustpan into a garbage bin in the corner, then turned to Hadley. "Would you like to sit a while and talk?"

"Yeah . . . I think I need to talk to someone. Thanks."

"I'll join you in the tearoom as soon as I put the broom away. Find a spot at one of the tables."

Rose filled a teapot with hot water and brought a selection of teas to the table.

"Thankfulness table?" Hadley read the words aloud. "Guess I picked the wrong table. I'm not feeling very thankful."

Rose filled Hadley's teacup, then placed a hand on her shoulder. "There's always something to be thankful for. Sometimes we just have to think about it for a bit. Tom seemed pretty angry—is he like that a lot?"

"Yeah, he does have a temper, but he's always sorry afterward."

"What do you think he meant when he told you not to let anyone get in your head?"

She sighed. "He said the same thing when I told him I was going to go talk to Pastor Dalton. He thinks I'm going to be brainwashed or something."

"Is he referring to your decision about the baby?"

"Yeah. He says we've already made the decision. I keep telling him I'm not sure anymore. Every day I think more about my baby—whether it's a boy or a girl, who he or she will look like—" She rubbed her hands over her face. "Last night I opened your Bible on the nightstand and read a verse in the book of Matthew—I think it was Jesus talking, and He said He longed to gather the children like a hen gathers her chicks under her wings." She laughed shakily. "Do they do that? Anyway, it sounded so nice. So loving."

Rose turned her chair toward Hadley and held her hand. "Oh, honey, what do you think God was saying to you then?"

"I think—I think I'm like that mother hen and . . . and I need to protect my chick." She placed both hands on her belly and rubbed gently. "I can't cause any harm to my baby—I just *can't*. I won't. I know Tom will be angry about it, but my baby is more important."

She lifted her chin and looked up at Rose, a determined look on her face. "Could we talk to Pastor Dalton about adoption? I'm ready. Would you go with me?"

"I would be honored. Would you like me to call and see if he's available now?"

"Yes. I think I made up my mind last night, but this made me sure. I know it's the best thing to do. It's what I have to do . . . so my baby can have a good home . . . and a mom and a dad."

Rose stepped away to make the call. When she returned, she was smiling. "We can meet him in an hour. You go get freshened up, and I'll finish what I'm doing here."

Hadley picked up a marker from the basket on the table. "I will—right after I make a note here. I do have something to be thankful for, don't I?"

"Yes, you do." Rose said with a big hug.

The girl spoke the words quietly as she wrote, "Thank you, God, for showing me the way." She added her initials and date, then made her way back to the cottage.

Rose let Libby know she'd be out for a while, then she followed Hadley out the door. She stopped in the garden to pray. "Oh, Lord, You are always faithful. Thank You for leading Hadley to the right verse that would speak to her heart. Amen."

Rose and Shannon both were busy arranging bouquets at the

counter Saturday morning when Shannon's cell rang. "Hi, Claire. I've been thinking about you. I'm working at Rose's; can I call you back in an hour?" A few words more and she disconnected.

Rose looked her way. "It's okay if you want to take a break now and call her back, Shannon. We aren't busy. How is Claire? Has she been back to visit recently?"

"Thanks, but I want to be free to talk for a while. She's lost another baby, their third one. I can't imagine how hard it is for her and Mark."

"Oh, my. I'm so sorry—unimaginable pain. The poor dear. I will pray for her and her husband."

Shannon laid her snippers and flowers on the counter. "I've been praying for God's will for my life a lot too. I've decided to see Andrew once a week, as long as things go well and so far, so good."

Rose put down the container she was gluing shells onto. "I hope you're being cautious and guarding your heart from further hurt, my dear."

"Same thing my mom said. I put up a huge wall at first because I didn't want to get hurt, but I do believe he's changed. He's trying."

"Well, I hope he's sincere. You've shared about his controlling behavior in the past—that doesn't change easily, so be cautious. God will answer your prayer about showing you His will."

"I know—I'm trying to be realistic. When we're together, it seems like the way things were when we were first married."

Rose looked at her, a concerned expression on her face. "He's on his best behavior with you right now. Time will tell, dear, time will tell. Give it time."

"I'm slowing things down. I think he's hoping to move the relationship quicker though, but I've told him I need time."

They moved to other topics as they continued working side by side for the next several minutes. The shop was quiet except for their conversation.

Both women looked up as the bell over the door announced a

customer. Max. Rose didn't miss Shannon's reaction as the newspaperman approached the counter. *She doesn't even know how much she likes him. I'm not sure if that's good or bad.*

At the counter, Max pulled a large framed picture out of a bag and handed it to Rose. "Something you might like to hang in your shop," he said with a beaming smile.

She stopped to admire the double-matted enlargement of the newspaper article. "Oh, Max, this is so thoughtful. Thank you." She turned to look at the wall behind the counter. "I'm going to hang it right here, where everyone can see. Oh, I love it!"

Max grinned, then turned to look at Shannon. "The pretty model in the photo is a nice addition to the shop, too, isn't she?"

"The prettiest," Rose agreed, observing Shannon's delicate blush. With a sly wink, she said, "I'm going to the back to get a nail and hammer. I'm sure you don't need me here. In fact, why don't you two go get a cup of tea. It's time for Shannon's break anyway."

"Oh, you're subtle, aren't you?" Shannon laughed.

"You bet." Rose grinned as she hurried away.

Max and Shannon collected their favorite teas and muffins, then found a table in the Tea Cozy.

"I was hoping you were still volunteering for Rose," he said as he pulled out a chair for her. "I've missed you."

"I've missed you too." Her smile was not as bright as usual. It made him a little nervous, especially when she rattled on, changing the subject. "What are you working on now since the article's been published?"

"I still have two more shop owners to interview, then I'll be switching to sports for a while. How's everything going with you?"

She shrugged. "Not much news at work; same old, same old."

She didn't look at him as she continued. "Andrew and I have had a few dates . . . I'm trying to sort things out."

Tread lightly, lightly. "I hope he's treating you right." He peered into her eyes, trying to get a read on her emotions.

"He is. I haven't held anything back—I'm telling him exactly where I stand and what I expect. We've got a lot more ground to cover, though."

He set his cup on the table and reached for her hand. "My feelings for you have not changed, Shannon. I'm giving you the time you need to assess the situation and your future. But I miss you terribly." *So much for treading lightly. Oh well.* "I can't say it's been a breeze on my end."

"I know, Max. I'm sorry about this. I don't know how to make it any easier."

"It's okay. I'd rather you be sure. Anyway, I want you to know, I'm here for you—anywhere, anytime. Just say the word. I've said it before—you're worth the wait. And I mean it sincerely." A rueful smile tipped his lips as he looked at her. "I never thought of myself as a patient man, but in this case, I'll wait patiently."

She squeezed his fingers quickly, then pulled her hand away. "Thank you, Max. It's a gift, and I truly appreciate it. Not many men would be so patient under these circumstances."

"Anyone who is in love with you would be patient." He studied her face for a moment. "Your happiness is the most important thing. But I don't want to make things more difficult for you, so I'm gonna leave it there." He was starting to get emotional, so it was time to leave. He pushed his chair back. "Thanks for chatting with me. I hope we can talk again soon."

"Yes, I hope so too."

"Bye . . . for now." He left her at the table and walked out to the counter, where he paused to say goodbye to Rose.

Shannon watched him leave, her heart in turmoil. A tear threatened, but she swiped it away. *God, I hate being in this situation. One minute I think I'm in love with Andrew, then I see Max and think I'm in love with him. I need clarity.*

She straightened the tablecloth, took a deep breath, and headed back out to the shop. Rose was at the counter, looking at the article again. "Wasn't it nice of Max to have this framed for me? It's a beautiful display. He's very thoughtful, isn't he?"

"Yes, he is." Shannon paused, but the words inside weren't going to stay there. "Okay—since no one's here, I'm just going to get this out. How can I be in love with both Max and Andrew?" A burst of nervous energy had her rearranging the countertop. She was *not* going to cry. "What's wrong with me, Rose? I'm so conflicted, and I hate it. I need this to be black and white, and it's anything but."

"You know me well enough, dear, to know I speak my mind. I believe you know which one you are truly in love with. Listen to your heart and your mind—both at the same time. Hearts can be fickle sometimes, and wishful thinking can cause a lot of heartache—I know that from experience." She reached to pat Shannon's hand. "Ask God to reveal the truth to you."

"I *am* asking God for that, and for clarity. But . . . Andrew says all the right things."

Rose nodded. "Have you thought maybe they are *too* right?"

"What do you mean?"

"He knows what you *want* to hear, doesn't he? But how does he respond when you ask about the hard things, the things you need to talk about?"

Shannon opened her mouth, closed it. Thought for a moment.

"He doesn't want to talk about the baby. I thought it was because he was embarrassed, ashamed of what he'd done."

"Look for red flags, Shannon. Ask God to show you any deception that might be present. Andrew doesn't have a particularly good track record in the truth department, does he?"

"No, he doesn't. I think I've let my emotions cover up a lot. When I think about it . . . you're right. There were red flags, and I didn't address them. But I need to."

"His reaction when you bring up the difficult subjects will show you where his heart is—whether he is placing you above his own needs and desires. If he's really changed, my dear, you will see humility, contriteness, and repentance for what he's done. There's more to reconciliation than making you happy in the moment."

"That's true. I'm so glad you're in my life, Rose. You have a lot of wisdom. Thank you."

"I've lived a lot more years than you have, young lady, and I've learned a few things along the way." She gave Shannon's shoulders a quick squeeze. "Now, let's get these last two arrangements finished before you have to leave. I'll be right back."

She stepped into the cooler for a few stems, leaving Shannon alone to think over their conversation.

Chapter Sixteen ❧

Andrew made the trip back to Shelton the next Sunday, meeting Shannon at four o'clock at the Chinese restaurant. He watched her climb out of her car and walk toward the door. With a last quick glance in the rearview mirror, he smoothed his hair and checked the rugged look of his scruffy beard. He'd noted her reaction to it the last time they were together. He'd be keeping that for a while. No doubt the attraction was still strong. He grinned at his reflection, then hopped out of his car, and met her on the sidewalk.

"Shannon, you look lovely. Your sweater makes those emerald eyes pop."

"Thank you." Her smile was soft.

"Should we start with a pupu platter? We have a few hours before the movie starts."

"Perfect."

"So, how was your week?"

"Mmm. Did I already tell you? I got some sad news about Claire and Mark—they lost another baby, their third miscarriage."

"Yeah, I heard about that at the club, one of Mark's golf partners. Must be really tough for both of them."

"I can't imagine what they've been through. It's hard enough not being able to get pregnant. Imagine losing one."

Yeah, imagine. The server lit the flame on the platter and took their orders.

"So . . . tell me about this place where you've been volunteering."

He listened while Shannon talked about Rose and the Amaryllis. He laughed when she described the broken containers but sobered up quickly when she protested.

"No, they're really cool, Andrew. I guess it does sound strange if you haven't seen them. When my neighbor first took me there, she said it was a magical place. And it is—Rose is charismatic and charming. Everyone in town loves her. Her shop is an experience, really."

"Well, maybe I can check it out sometime."

She stopped and looked at him, the expression on her face changing. "Yeah," she said. "I haven't asked you. How did you know where I was? How did you find my job?"

"Oh, I uh, I ran into one of your old coworkers on the golf course. He told me you'd been in an accident, too, so I had to see you. Needed to make sure you were okay. Luckily, he knew where you were."

She looked at him for a moment, then relented. "Well, it was a little creepy—you just showing up."

"I'm sorry." He held back a laugh as he thought of her expression when she'd seen him. "You were pretty freaked out, actually. I thought you were going to call the police for a minute there. I'd never seen you so angry before—and I hope I never do again."

He raised an eyebrow. "This Rose—why doesn't she pay you?"

"I offered to volunteer. She uses most of her resources to help women who need help getting back on their feet—for various reasons. She's like, everyone's unofficial counselor. She's a wise lady."

"I'll have to meet this amazing woman. What about next weekend? I'd love to see your apartment and check out the Loughton Valley area. We could spend the whole day together."

He watched a range of emotions play over her expressive face. For a minute he thought she was going to turn him down. Finally, she smiled. "Sure, that would be fun. What time could you be at my apartment?"

"How about Saturday at ten? I can't do Sunday next week. It would give us some good time together."

Her mouth twisted as she thought about that. "Okay. I'll have to let Rose know I won't be working that day, but we can pop in so you can meet her and see the shop. If the weather's good, there are some hiking trails in a nearby state park I've been wanting to explore."

"That sounds perfect." He checked the time on his phone. "Oops, we better get going, or we'll miss the beginning of the movie." He took care of the check, then talked her into riding with him to the theater and then to a bakery and coffee shop for dessert.

When they were finished, he drove her back to her car. He shut off the motor, then turned toward her. He reached over and took her hand. He looked closely into her eyes.

"Shannon, every time I have to say goodbye to you, it gets harder. All I think about on the drive home is you—everything about you. It's like the world stops, and you're all that matters. You know, I think about you every day. And I'm the happiest when I'm with you."

She bit her lip, still not ready to commit. "We need to be patient, Andrew. This is going to take some time—but we're moving in the right direction."

His fingers tightened around hers for a moment. He took a breath, then smiled at her. "I'm trying, but it's not easy. Could I have a goodbye kiss?" She leaned into him, and after a long embrace and kiss in the car, they said goodbye.

Shannon's phone buzzed while she was out walking Willow after work on Monday. A smile lit her face as she answered. "Hi, Claire."

The excitement in her voice spoke volumes. "Mark and I are pinching ourselves actually. We kept it pretty quiet, but we've been working with a local adoption agency. We got a call about a baby that we may be able to adopt soon. It's like a dream!"

"I am so excited for you, both of you." Shannon's voice thrilled with happiness.

"Oh, thank you."

"Wow! That's amazing. You and I will have to go shopping. Auntie Shannon needs to buy a few things for this very special baby."

"It truly is a miracle."

Saturday dawned clear and sunny, so Shannon dressed warmly for the hike and filled her backpack. Andrew rang the doorbell at exactly ten o'clock.

"Wow, you have really improved in the area of promptness." She greeted him with a quick hug.

"Been working on it—I know it's important to you."

At the sound of a strange voice, Willow crowded up beside Shannon. Andrew reached down toward the dog, but she pulled away, her teeth bared.

"Whoa!" he exclaimed. "Looks like she's pretty protective of you."

Shannon's hand was on the dog's collar as she soothed the animal. "Willow, it's okay. He's friendly." She looked up at Andrew, her eyes wide. "I'm sorry—I've never seen her act this way."

The dog sniffed his leg, then his hand. Finally, with an expressive snort, Willow walked away, letting him into the apartment. Shannon apologized again.

"Don't worry about it. At least you know she'll keep you safe." He looked around. "This place is really nice, Shannon. You did a good job."

She laughed. "It came furnished. Most of the things I had were broken in the accident. Anyway, thanks. I like it here. Would you like anything to eat before we leave?"

"Nope—I'm good."

"I packed some snacks for the hike and a cooler with some water. I told Rose we'd stop by first."

Shannon pointed out her favorite shops and cafés as he drove through town. A space was open right in front of the Amaryllis. He parked the car then hurried around to Shannon's side. The surprise on her face gave him a sense of satisfaction.

The bell over the shop door jingled and he held open the door, letting her pass while his eyes made a quick survey of the shop.

"You must be Andrew. I'm Rose. Welcome."

"Hello, Rose." They shook hands. "I've been looking forward to meeting you and seeing where Shannon spends her Saturdays."

"Oh, I appreciate the time she gives me, so much. She's a great help, and the customers love her."

"I'm sure they do. There's a lot to love about her." He placed an arm around Shannon's shoulders. She let him pull her close.

The blue and gold vase behind the antique cash register caught his eye. When he commented on it, Rose explained the kintsugi process and how it was an inspiration for her shop.

When she was done, Shannon took his hand. "Let's walk around—I'll show you some of the other items Rose has repaired." They walked slowly from aisle to aisle as she described several pieces on the shelves. "Rose loves repairing damaged items and making them beautiful again. I was dusting in here last week, admiring some of them, and I thought about how we're kind of like these containers. Our relationship was damaged and broken . . . but here we are, trying to repair it and make it better than it was before."

"I like the comparison." He smiled. "She certainly has a unique concept with the shop. Do these things really sell? I mean, they are broken."

Shannon laughed. "You'd be surprised. I see them at work and around town in other shops—they're everywhere. People love giving bouquets in her creatively repaired containers." She pointed to the punchbowl. "They bring her all kinds of scraps and broken pieces of things to use."

He shook his head, still trying to wrap his mind around the concept. She did seem to have a working business, though. They returned to the counter and chatted with Rose for a few minutes more. Andrew noticed the framed picture of the article, recognized Shannon in the photo, and moved closer to examine it. "Looks like you're a local celebrity too," he said.

She wrinkled her nose a bit, and that made him curious. He turned back to the piece and read the byline aloud. "Maxwell Harrington. Is that the guy—"

"Yes," Shannon said.

"Hmmm . . . I think I'm jealous." He looked closer at the small photo next to Max's name. His smile was tight. Shannon's face was slightly pink as she took his hand.

"Come on," she urged. "Let me show you the rest of the shop. You have to experience the Tea Cozy."

He followed her to the tearoom and looked around at the tables. "This is a strange place," he muttered, "but I guess I see why you like it."

"I love it here," she declared. "I thought we could buy a few scones for later; they're delicious." She chose four and placed them in a bag. Then she walked back to the counter to pay for them.

"I'll get these," he said, taking them from her hand. "Rose,

Shannon is very fond of you. I'm glad she has such a nice friend and a great place to spend some time. It was nice to meet you."

"Nice to meet you too, Andrew. Thanks for stopping by. You kids have a great hike today. It feels like spring out there, doesn't it?"

"Finally," Shannon replied. "I'll see you next Saturday."

As he drove to the state park, she told him about Mark and Claire and the possibility of adopting soon.

"You can't imagine how excited they are. I'm so happy for them."

"Yes," he replied, but his mind was elsewhere. "So, are you still seeing that Max guy? That article was pretty recent."

She bristled. "We aren't dating, if that's what you're getting at. We met in the shop; he took a few pictures; we got something to eat. I'm not comfortable with you pressuring me."

"I'm not pressuring you. I'm asking a question." He worked to control the irritation in his voice.

"Your tone is making me feel pressured. Let's drop the subject, please."

He shrugged. "He's a handsome guy. I just want to know if I have competition." He reached for her hand, but she pulled it away.

"Andrew. The only competition you have is you. Everything depends on you, and I'll tell you right now, you aren't doing so good. I asked you to drop it."

"Okay, okay—don't get so riled up. Your attitude makes me think there's more to the story than you're telling me."

Her face darkened. "I told you, we aren't dating." She pulled her cell phone out of her purse and began checking emails. "I'm not going to argue about it."

"Okay, subject closed." They rode in silence until the park entrance sign was in sight. "Do we park in this first lot?"

"No, drive through. There's another lot up a little farther; it's closer to the trailhead."

They hiked for about thirty minutes, mostly in silence. When they reached the lake, they sat on a bench facing the water and ate their scones.

It was time to make peace. "You still seem ticked," he said. "Let's not make a big deal out of this. You said you're not dating, so I shouldn't have pressed the issue. I'm sorry."

"If you'd pay attention, you'd notice I haven't asked you if you're dating anyone."

True. "Well, if you're asking now—the answer is no. Not since I saw you in the parking lot at your job. I knew then you were the only one for me." He tried unsuccessfully again to hold her hand.

"Okay, then let's move on." She stood and started walking.

The full trek around the lake took three hours, with one more break halfway around. By the time they reached the car again, her attitude had thawed. They discussed where to go for an early dinner and decided to grill steaks at her apartment instead.

He started the car, then reached over to give her a quick hug. "Shannon, this has been good; the hike was a great idea. I hope I didn't spoil the day for you."

"You didn't spoil it. You were coming across jealous and possessive. I'm hoping that won't come up again."

"It won't. I trust you."

She nodded. "We're trusting each other. Ready for some ice cream?"

❦

"Hello . . ." Rose answered her cell while arranging three bouquets with Shannon at the counter Saturday morning. "No!" The tool she was holding clattered to the counter. Shannon looked up, surprised, as Rose continued. "I told you, *not* on this number. I'll go to the house and call you back. I'm sorry . . . I understand, but—"

Realizing Shannon was listening, Rose stopped talking and moved to the window, listening to the caller. Her voice was quieter the next time she spoke. "I understand, dear, but I can't discuss it here. I will have to call you back."

With a deep sigh of frustration, she listened intently again. "I know . . . I know . . . but it's not safe. I can't talk on this line. I'll call you back in five minutes."

"Shannon, please finish up. I'll be back." The sharp tone of her voice was one Shannon had not heard before, and she watched, concerned, as Rose scurried off to the cottage. Twenty minutes later she returned, eyes red and lips pursed.

"Is everything okay?" Shannon asked.

"Yes, everything's fine." She stepped briskly to the cooler, then returned with an armful of flowers to add finishing touches on the bouquets. When she finished, she gave the nearest arrangement a pat, then pushed it across the counter toward Shannon. "The customers should be in soon for their orders. Can you cash them out? I'm going to put another batch of muffins in the oven." She tried unsuccessfully to cover a sniff.

"Of course. Rose, I—"

"It's fine, Shannon. I'm fine." She moved off to the tearoom with a frenetic energy.

Shannon had never seen her upset before—and when she returned, she seemed distant and preoccupied. She bustled about the shop for the next hour, straightening and organizing in both rooms, keeping busy.

Shannon kept a watchful eye on her. *She's not herself.* Worry mixed with curiosity as the morning wore on. At eleven o'clock, Rose returned to the counter and reminded Shannon her shift was over.

"Thank you for your help, as always. Oh, and I meant to tell you, Libby has found a full-time job in an accountant's office in town and I hired a replacement—Madelaine. She's coming in this afternoon to fill out paperwork and will start next week. She's very sweet. You will like her."

"Good for Libby," Shannon exclaimed. "I'll give her a call to congratulate her. I look forward to meeting Madelaine. If you need anyth—" The look on Rose's face rerouted her words. "I'll see you next week, Rose. I hope it's a good one for you."

"Yes, dear. We'll see you next week."

Chapter Seventeen 🌹

Shannon had been thinking about Rose's advice to introduce the hard topics, so on Sunday after dinner while they were relaxing on the couch, she calmly stated, "I would like to meet Sienna."

Andrew fidgeted uncomfortably. "Umm, don't you think that's a little premature? I mean, we're still working things out and all." He cleared his throat.

"But she's an important part of your life now, and if we're going forward, I should spend some time with her too, don't you think? Get to know her?" *I will not second-guess that odd reaction.*

"Let me think about it." He hesitated, then squeezed her shoulders. "Since I only get to see you once a week, I want you *all* to myself when we're together."

"Well, it's important to me. I hope you reconsider. I mean, it's kinda weird—the only photo you've shown me is her newborn picture. Don't you have anything recent? Not even on your phone? Seems like you'd want to be showing her off to everyone."

He flashed her a look she couldn't interpret, then said, "You know I'm not much of a photo-taker. Besides, when I'm with you, you're my focus." He finished with his best toothy smile.

On the way to the kitchen to get their dessert, she couldn't shake his reaction. *What is he not telling me? Something isn't right. Nah, I'm probably reading more into it than I should be. He's right, we need to focus on us.*

They finished dessert, and he scooted closer to her on the couch. "Hon, it's getting harder to say goodbye each time I see you. I think about you all week long. I have one of my favorite pictures of you on my desk—that one on the beach in Maui . . . remember how special that week was?"

"I do—our fifth anniversary and my first trip to Hawaii. I'm glad you saved some pictures. Crazy me, I didn't save mine."

"What?"

"I got rid of everything not long after I moved here."

He was quiet for a minute, then said jokingly, "Hmmm, sounds like you were erasing me completely from your life."

Shannon didn't answer, she just shrugged.

His face was unreadable again as he declared, "Well, I couldn't do that. I knew we'd be together again some day. And look at us, here we are." He reached for her hand and held it tightly. "I'm thankful we can pick up the pieces. And I think we'll be better than before. Don't you?"

"Sometimes. But it's still going to take a lot of w—"

"Let's go back."

"Back? To Maui?"

"Yeah. Let's take a week and get to know each other again in our favorite spot in the world. You and me, no distractions. What do you say?" He put his arm around her, pulling her closer.

"No, that wouldn't be right. We're not married anymore."

"Okay then—let's get married there. We already had a big wedding; we don't need another one. A private ceremony on the beach, what do you think?" He stood up, then knelt beside the couch. "Shannon Amelia Enright, will you marry me—again?"

"You can't be serious?" She chuckled nervously.

"One hundred percent serious. Couldn't be more serious. I need you in my life—every day, not just on Sundays. My life's not complete without you. I love you and I want us to be together again, as a married couple. Don't you?" He shifted back onto the couch and snuggled close again.

"It's too soon, Andrew. I need more time to be sure what we have is real. That it will last this time. Two minutes ago you said we were still working things out, and now you're talking about getting married quickly. Neither one of us knows what we want right now."

"Okay, my love. I guess my proposal bombed. I'll suffer through another week until we can be together again." He whisked her up into his arms and held her tightly. "I don't think it's too soon, but I'll respect your feelings."

"Oh, you're so dramatic sometimes," she said. "But it is getting late, and you've got a long drive. You should probably head back home. We'll talk about this later."

He protested a moment more, then stood, and together, they went to the door.

"Have a safe drive back," she said, handing him his jacket.

He scooped her up for a last quick kiss. "Okay, goodnight. See you next weekend."

Thinking about their Maui anniversary trip as she was pulling up the covers, she closed her eyes and pictured lying on the gorgeous beach with the love of her life—happy, secure, content. She wanted those feelings back again. *Has he really changed? Or is it wishful thinking?* Deliberately, she pushed away thoughts of his strange actions earlier. "No, tonight, I'm just going to think about the good," she murmured. Willow jumped up and snuggled next to her. She gave the dog a sleepy hug. "And yes, that includes you, Willow," she said as she drifted off with happy memories.

The next day, she remembered to give Libby a call. "Hey, Libby, it's Shannon. Rose told me about your new job. Congratulations."

"Thanks. It took a little longer than I hoped, but I'm really excited about the job. So far I love it. It feels so good to have a full-time job again, with benefits."

"I'm sure. Rose and I will miss you though. Hopefully, you'll stop by on Saturdays once in a while."

"Of course I will. Hey . . . one thing before you go . . . remember the broken frame and strange photo I told you about? And Rose's odd reaction, then it disappeared."

"Yeah."

"Well, I love her, and she's been very kind and gracious to me. But things felt different after that. She was distant with me. But there were a few more strange things too. Has the police chief ever come to the shop while you were there?"

"No, I've never seen the police there."

"The chief came several times recently, and every time, Rose went straight to the cottage with him. She always seemed uncomfortable too. At first I thought it had to do with one of the women she was helping, but then no one was staying at the cottage. I asked her about it once—she was very evasive and nervous. Something's not right, and I don't know what it is. Have you ever gotten a similar sense?"

"No," Shannon lied. "I'm sure there's a logical explanation for everything. She's a wonderful lady."

"I'm not saying she isn't. I just . . . she's being very mysterious about something, and whatever it is was starting to come between us. It's still troubling me. Oh, well. I'll let it go, there's nothing I can do about it now anyway."

"That's true," Shannon said. "I'm happy you like your new job and I hope to see you again soon."

"I'll stop by for sure. Maybe we can have coffee after your shift."

"Yes, let's get together. Have a great week in your new job."

"Thanks."

What would involve the police? Shannon didn't like to think about questioning Rose's honesty or sincerity . . . whatever was causing the suspicions. She decided to leave it, like Libby had said.

Friday night, Claire called with big news. "We're going to have a daughter!"

"Really?" Shannon squealed. "That's awesome."

"Yep. And her name will be Charlotte Amelia."

"Oh, Claire, I'm so honored."

"I always loved your middle name, and Charlotte was my grandmother's name. It's perfect."

"That's so special. I can't wait to meet her, and I'm so happy for you. I'd like to give you a shower. I'll talk to Mom, I'm sure we can have it at their house once Miss Charlotte makes her grand appearance."

"Oh, how wonderful. Thank you. It means a lot to me."

"My pleasure. You must be on cloud nine. I'm sure there's a lot to do in the next few months."

"Oh yeah—a lot, but I'm thoroughly enjoying every moment. We're going to paint the nursery tomorrow; I can't wait to get started."

"Send some pics when you finish painting."

They chattered for a while, but Shannon was feeling antsy. She wanted to ask Claire some questions . . . but part of her didn't want to ask either. Finally, she decided to just go for it. "Hey, do you have a few more minutes to talk?"

"Sure, I always have time for you. What's up?"

"Last weekend, Andrew asked me to marry him. Is he crazy or what?"

"Wow! What a shocker."

"I know. He asked me to go to Maui with him for a week first, and when I said no, then he started talking about getting married there, on the beach—like right away. Really caught me off guard."

"I'd say. How do you feel about it?"

"Well, it's still too soon. But the way things have been going, I can see us together again. He's changed—much more attentive and loving—not all self-absorbed like he could be in the past. He did get jealous once though," she chuckled. "He saw a photo of Max in the article about Rose's shop, but I told him we weren't dating anymore. He reassured me he isn't dating anyone either, so we're on the same page. I really feel . . . I think I can trust him again."

There was an awkward pause.

"Are you still there?"

"I'm here . . . sorry."

"If you need to go, we can talk again later."

"Ummm . . . no. Well, Mark and I saw Andrew at a restaurant last week." Claire paused. "With a woman."

"What?" Shannon gasped as her mind flashed back to the day she'd found out about Andrew's affair.

"I'm sorry, Shannon. I didn't know whether to tell you. Honestly, I didn't think your relationship was going to get serious again, but when you said he asked you to marry him—well, you have a right to know. Neither of us had seen her before. They had to walk past our table as they left, and he seemed uncomfortable when he saw us. He introduced her as a coworker."

Shannon's voice quivered. "If he said she was a coworker, then I believe him. Thanks for telling me. I know you're looking out for me. I'll talk to him about it—I'm sure it was all innocent." She was trying desperately to reel in her emotions, but it was time to end the call.

"I hope so."

"Me too. Well, I'd better let you go. We'll talk later." Emotions were swirling; she could barely speak.

"Okay, bye."

Is he lying to me again? A coworker, at a restaurant? Could it be innocent? Lela was a coworker, too.

She debated with herself, recalling their recent conversations about honesty and trust. He had been so convincing. *I believe him. Well, I did.* Her stomach was in knots, but there were no tears— only anger and confusion. *I'll ask him Sunday. I need to see his reaction to tell if he's lying.*

Her mind was a million miles away as she stared at the TV, unable to focus. She picked up a book to try to read—and his letter fell out. She trembled as she read it again. *Has this all just been a game? What are you doing, Andrew? What am I doing?*

She couldn't shake Claire's words. All week they replayed in her head. She even had a few mini meltdowns in the bathroom at work. Over and over, she wondered if she'd really be able to tell if he was being truthful. She was looking forward to Saturday and helping at the Amaryllis. The busyness and customers there always provided a distraction.

When she arrived, Rose asked if she'd help train Madelaine. She was happy to do so, and they hit it off great. They were close in age, both divorced, and neither had children. When Madelaine asked if she was dating anyone, she replied yes without providing details.

She realized later that had revealed an inner lack of confidence about the future of her relationship with Andrew.

Sunday morning, as she waited for Andrew's arrival, anxiety rolled back in. By the time he arrived at 11 o'clock, cheery and animated, she was feeling quite ill.

"What's on the agenda today?" He asked with a hug.

She pushed him away, wanting to see his face. "First on the agenda is this: are you dating someone else?"

"Whoa! That came out of left field. I told you I'm not dating anyone but you."

"I talked to Claire."

"Oh, that. Can we at least sit down and talk about it?" He motioned toward the couch and they sat down, but Shannon kept space between them. "Sheesh! You jumped all over me as soon as I entered the door."

"So answer the question. Who was she?"

"I had a project at work, and a coworker and I worked late to meet the deadline. When we realized the time, we decided to get dinner together. That's all it was. It certainly wasn't a date—more like finishing up a business meeting." He gave her a smile and scooted closer. "Do you still not trust me?"

Repelling his advance, she replied. "I don't know. If you'd told me about it, then I wouldn't be questioning you now. Look—you're the one who had *secrets* in the past. You have to understand, this resurrects those old negative, painful feelings."

"I'm sorry. I can see now how you could be upset. I didn't tell you because there wasn't anything to it—I didn't think it would cause a problem. I'm sorry. Believe me, there's nothing more to tell. It was one isolated event. Are we okay now?"

"There can't be *any* secrets, Andrew. I told you early on, honesty is crucial if we're going to restore this relationship."

"Fine, but as I recall, you didn't tell me about having dinner with what's-his-name, Max, until I questioned you about it at Rose's shop," he said sternly. "So was that your secret?"

"Don't deflect this on me. That was not the same thing, and you know it. I can't keep finding out things from other people. If you aren't going to be completely honest and transparent with me, this isn't going to work."

He sighed. "Really, Shannon. It's nothing. Besides, do you think I would have asked you to marry me last week if I was seeing someone else?"

"I suppose not—I *hope* not. Let's take Willow for a walk around the lake—I need fresh air. And then we can go to lunch."

"So, are we good? I hope our day hasn't been ruined already."

"I had a lot of doubts this week, but I'm choosing to trust you. I hope the trust is merited." She looked sternly at him, then fastened the leash on Willow, who still wasn't warming up to him.

"That's all I ask."

They stopped to rest on a bench beside the lake. Andrew hesitated, then turned toward her. "So . . . I brought you something," he said, pulling a small box from his pocket. "I pictured giving it to you differently, but—here."

"What's this?" Surprised, she lifted the top of the box. "Ohh . . . it's beautiful." The heart-shaped pendant necklace glistened in the sunlight.

"It's diamonds and white gold. You made it clear you're not ready for an engagement ring, so when I saw it this week, I thought it would be perfect. Something you could wear every day to remind you of my love."

"It's gorgeous," she breathed, holding the pendant closer and observing the facets as they sparkled in the sun's rays. "But I'm not sure I should accept such an expensive gift. Especially after the way I greeted you. I'm sorry."

"Don't worry about that. After everything I've put you through, I should be showering you with gifts. I'm sorry I didn't think about it sooner. It's a small token of my love for you."

"Thank you, Andrew. I don't know what to say. It's lovely."

"Just say you love it." He fastened it on her neck, and she wanted to believe his warm embrace and kiss were genuine assurances of his love.

"I do love it—a lot. Thank you."

"I want you to be happy."

They finished their casual walk around the lake, had a late lunch, and watched a movie at the theater. That evening, he cooked steaks on the grill. Shannon desperately wanted to believe he was being truthful—because she couldn't bear to think of the alternative.

Before he left, he asked again, "Are we okay? I don't want there to be an issue between us."

"Yes, I trust you."

"Great. I'll give you a call tomorrow. That necklace sure looks good on you." He gave her one last kiss before leaving.

She took the necklace off and admired it more closely. She counted twenty diamonds outlining the heart shape. *Jeez! It's beautiful.*

❦

"Rose, could I talk with you sometime this morning," Shannon asked while checking in for her shift on Saturday.

"Of course, dear. Let me finish this order and then I'll have some free time. Madelaine's coming in at ten."

"Thanks." Shannon unpacked a recent delivery of silk flowers, organized them by color, and took them to the supply room in back. *Why am I still questioning whether he's being honest? I can't shake it.*

Rose peeked inside the room. "I'm all set now." Noticing the sparkle at Shannon's throat, she remarked, "My goodness, what a beautiful necklace. I haven't seen you wear it before."

"It's from Andrew, he gave it to me last weekend."

"It's quite stunning. Now, would you like to talk in the cottage?"

"Sure, thanks." Shannon stopped in the garden to admire some of the spring flowers. "Soon everything will be blooming. I love your gardens."

"Thank you, dear. Every year I enjoy them more also."

Taking a seat in the living room, Rose asked, "Now what's on your mind?"

"Well, remember when you told me about amaryllis bulbs

needing time to refresh so they can bloom again? I was so hopeful it could be me too. I love the illustration—but I'm questioning if I can really bloom, if you know what I mean. I still have so many doubts about a future with Andrew."

"After what you've been through, that's understandable. You were wounded deeply, and those wounds take time to heal. But always remember, *who* you are has never changed, Shannon. God has given you gifts, attributes, abilities and so much more—to bloom as He has designed."

"But I feel like I won't be able to completely trust him again." She paused. "I found out he had dinner with a woman. He said she was a coworker. Claire and Mark saw them at a restaurant, and I confronted him about it. He said they worked late on a project and finished their discussion over dinner. I want to believe him, but I can't shake this uneasy feeling."

"It's because he's betrayed you already. He's caused a lack of trust. He'll have to earn your trust back, dear. Is he willing? It's a slow process."

"He says he is. He asked me to marry him, but I'm definitely not ready."

"Do you believe your relationship should progress according to *your* timetable, as you trust your instincts?"

"That's just it. I'm so confused. I have such strong feelings for him, but I'm not sure it's love—not like the love I had for him before. I trusted him completely when we were married—never once questioned his faithfulness." She was getting teary. "Then, when the bomb hit, I felt like I would never be able to trust him or anyone else, ever again. I took our marriage vows seriously, so when he contacted me again, I thought I should give him a chance—see if he really had changed."

"Because of the pain, you are being cautious. You're guarding your heart, and it's a good thing. When we trust someone who's hurt us deeply, we're opening ourselves up to the possibility of being hurt again. But living always requires a level of trust without guarantees. I don't want you to be hurt again either, dear."

"Yeah, but it's hard because I want to believe him and trust him. At the same time, all these little red flags keep waving around in my head. Is that normal?"

"Well, I would say there should be fewer red flags as you spend more time together. I hope he's sensitive to the insecurities he's caused and he's trying to reassure you of his faithfulness."

"I think it's me actually—I've become very insecure. I don't want to be, but I am."

"It takes time. Continue to ask God for discernment and guidance. He wants the best for you, and you will know."

"Thanks for talking with me—I really appreciate it." She looked around the room. "Your cottage is always so welcoming—I feel peaceful here."

"Thank you. You know I'm always available."

They walked back to the shop and Rose picked up a dormant potted amaryllis bulb and handed it to Shannon. "Take this home and watch the process unfold. Let it be a reminder—God is working even if you don't see a lot happening initially. Soon there will be a shoot or two, and it will grow straight and tall. Then the buds will appear, and the beautiful blossoms will emerge in all their glory. You'll see."

"Thank you. I'll enjoy it very much."

That afternoon, she placed the pot on the kitchen table, marveling how anything of beauty could come from the dead-looking, dried-up bulb. Then she began to think about the timing of the necklace—she hadn't received any gifts from him since they began dating again. Was it because Claire and Mark had seen him at the restaurant? Did he feel guilty? Was he worried how she would react? Was it a peace-offering, a genuine love gift . . . or another red flag? *How will I know?*

❧

Claire and Mark brought their new daughter home from the hospital in early June, three days after she was born. Two weeks later, Shannon returned home to host the baby shower. Her first stop was Claire's, to meet Charlotte.

"Here she is." Claire placed the baby in Shannon's arms.

"She's beautiful." Stroking the child's cheek, she marveled. "Look at all this curly black hair and these bright blue eyes and rosy cheeks. Oh, Claire, she's a doll. Hello, Miss Charlotte."

"The doctor said she is perfect. I still pinch myself from time to time. I can't believe how much I love her—from the very first moment I held her in my arms. God is so good."

With a bright smile, she led the way upstairs. "Come see the nursery."

Shannon admired the room—walls painted light pink with pink, yellow, and teal curtains, a white crib and dresser, and a child's rocker with the large teddy bear she had sent. "What a beautiful room. Charlotte is one blessed little girl."

"We are the ones who are blessed." She pulled out the scrapbook she'd started for Charlotte and showed her the photos and mementos she'd already collected in the few weeks since her daughter's birth. Claire's delight was uncontainable as she described each photo and happy moment.

Shannon was happy to make a special day for Claire, Mark, and sweet Charlotte, and the shower was a success. It felt good to connect with old friends once again, but there were awkward moments too, like when Andrew was mentioned. People didn't quite know what to say when they discovered she was dating him again. And then there were the bittersweet thoughts—everyone at the shower was married and most had children. Her own longing for a family resurfaced and she thought about Andrew . . . and Sienna . . . . She wondered what it would be like to have a stepdaughter.

Early the next Saturday morning, Shannon turned quickly toward the door as a familiar voice boomed, "Good morning, Rose."

"Why, Max! You've been a stranger lately. I'm so happy you stopped by. How have you been?"

"Busy. How's business here?" he said with a hug.

"Business is great, thanks to you. I'm grateful." She smiled.

"It was all my pleasure. I'm glad we could get some new customers for you. In fact, I was thinking we should advertise your shop on social media—get the word out to an even larger audience."

Rose recoiled slightly. "Oh, no. I think I have all the business I can handle right now. And I'm not into social media." She fidgeted nervously.

"I'd help you with the technical details. We could get you a wide circulation, maybe nationwide."

At the word *nationwide,* Rose actually stepped backward. "Oh, heavens, no. Not right now. Maybe sometime in the future."

"Okay, but at least give it some thought. You could expand your shipping business, that would be a good thing for sure."

Rose shook her head emphatically. "Thank you, but not now. Excuse me." She turned quickly to greet a customer who was waiting at the counter.

Shannon had watched the whole scene, but now she realized he was smiling at her. She couldn't stop looking at him as he walked toward her.

"Good morning, Shannon. How have you been?"

Slow down, heart! Man, that smile gets me every time. "Good. I'm good. It's nice to see you."

"D'you think Rose could do without you for a short break? I'd love to get some tea with you."

Apparently, Rose was watching them too. "Of course," she said. "You two go catch up."

Shannon set down the snipping tool she'd been using and led the way to the Tea Cozy. They chose their drinks and settled at an empty thankfulness table. She caught him looking again, only this time it wasn't really at her.

"That's a beautiful necklace you're wearing. Should I presume it's from Andrew?" His smile was a little crooked.

"Yes, a recent gift." She shifted awkwardly in her chair.

"So . . . things are going good with him?" He stopped, picked up his tea. "I'm sorry. If you don't want to answer, I'll understand. But the truth is, Shannon, I just can't stop thinking about you. I guess . . . I guess, selfishly, I'd like to know if I still have a chance."

She felt her cheeks flush warmly. She didn't know what to say, but after a brief moment of silence and a hasty sip of tea, she began. "Ah, Max. You're such a great guy. This is not fair to you. You'll make someone very happy, and you deserve to be happy."

"So it's a no?" He couldn't hide his disappointment. His usually smiling eyes took on a serious look, and his chest expanded with a deep sigh.

Is it? She didn't know.

"The truth is—I do still have feelings for you. Every time I see you, I know it. And I've missed you and I do think about all the great times we had together." She wiped a tear away. "I'm sorry, I don't know why I'm crying." Her cheeks must be bright red.

Max leaned toward her and looked into her eyes. "The last thing I want to do is make you sad. I'm sorry I put you in an awkward position. I'll drop the subject."

"No, maybe we do need to talk about it." She wiped the tears and sniffled, trying to regain her composure. "Andrew asked me to marry him again. I said no, but . . . I knew I wasn't ready. I still have doubts about the future of the relationship. Truthfully—I don't know if I can trust him."

"Whoa! Marriage, huh? He doesn't waste time. I understand the trust issue—I don't think I could ever trust my ex again, given the option. Obviously, you're the better person. You've been way more willing to try than I would have been."

Shannon waved away his words. "What I'm saying is, I don't think it's fair for you to be waiting for me to make up my mind. I thought I would know by now, and I don't. Some days it seems I'm more confused than ever. You should be dating." *Why did I say that?*

"No, I'll wait, Shannon. I told you before, waiting isn't a problem—you're worth it. I have to say I do feel helpless though. There isn't anything I can do to win you back. But I don't question how I feel about you."

"Max. I'm very flattered."

"It's all true. I fell in love with you, and I'm still in love with you. How could I date anyone else? Some day, when you tell me you're actually engaged, then I will *t-r-y* to move on."

A few tears seeped out. Shannon felt undeserving of his love yet honored, and she tried to lighten the moment. "You know, he was pretty jealous when he saw your picture in the article."

"Not half as jealous as I've been—he spends time with you, and I can't." His smile was back. "I'm just glad I haven't run into the two of you in town. That would be much harder."

"We've only been in town together once—he wanted to meet Rose and see the shop."

"Good, for me at least." He lowered his voice and spoke softly. "Hey, did you notice her reaction when I mentioned advertising on social media?"

"I did—she's definitely not comfortable with the idea."

"Yeah, it was the reaction I thought she would have since she didn't want her picture in the paper. I can't put my finger on why, but I think she's afraid of publicity. It really has me puzzled."

"Have you ever asked her about it?"

"Heck no! I don't want to offend her or make her uncomfortable. She's the sweetest lady I know. Besides you, of course." He winked.

"Whatever." She laughed. When they'd finished their tea, he walked her back to the counter.

"Thanks for talking with me. I do want the best for you. You're a highly intelligent woman, and I know you'll figure this all out and make the right decision—for you."

"Thanks, Max. I appreciate you very much."

He walked out the door, and to Shannon, it seemed like the sun had gone away. She was sure she was making a huge mistake, one she'd regret forever. She just didn't know which decision was the mistake.

Help me, Lord, please, she prayed. *I'm in such a mess. It's not fair to Max to drag this on and on, but I truly don't know. I think I love him, but I have to deal honorably with Andrew too. Show me the way, Lord. Please, show me the way.*

Chapter Eighteen

Shannon spent a restless night, worrying about the situation. By five the next morning, she'd decided to stop fighting and just get up. She grabbed a flashlight and took a surprised Willow out for a quick walk. Then she sat on the porch, sipping coffee and watching the sun rise. The chirping birds announced the start to a glorious early summer day.

But inside, she was restless. She'd spent the night praying and asking God for wisdom. Why couldn't she find peace? She couldn't get Max out of her mind. Shouldn't she be thinking about Andrew since he would be here soon? Was she being ungrateful? He'd given her a gorgeous, expensive diamond necklace—something any woman would be thrilled about. *What's wrong with me?*

Her cell rang and she went inside to see who it was. Andrew. She didn't answer it—whatever he wanted, they'd talk about when he arrived. She was hoping she could lose this blasé mood before then. She hadn't felt this uneasy since the first time they'd met after his letter—and she couldn't put her finger on why.

She got dressed, then took a second cup of coffee to the porch in an attempt to overcome a distinct drowsiness. Her sleepless night was going to make this day interesting. She and Andrew had plans to go an art fair in Lewsburg less than an hour away.

The doorbell rang and she stretched and yawned, then headed inside to answer it.

Andrew planted a big kiss on her lips and presented a bouquet of spring flowers. They were perfect for one of Rose's containers.

"Thank you, they're very pretty. I packed some drinks and snacks for the car. If we leave now, we should get there shortly after the fair opens."

Only small talk in the car—Shannon was quiet, but Andrew was more chatty than usual, mostly about his job. He did mention his parents, told her they had sent their regards and were hoping things were going well for them as a couple.

She almost laughed but managed to just raise an eyebrow instead. *I doubt that; they never made me feel welcome. I'm not looking forward to having them back in my life.*

A few artisans were still setting up their booths and displays when they arrived, but a large crowd of fairgoers had already gathered. Andrew held her hand as they walked, and Shannon imagined they must look like a happy couple to the world. *So why am I feeling this way inside?*

A squeeze from Andrew brought her attention back to him. "What kind of painting are you hoping to get for your apartment?" he asked.

"I don't know. I'll know when I see it—maybe a beach or a mountain scene. Something relaxing . . . a peaceful painting."

Halfway around the circle of exhibits, he spotted a painting in the distance. "I think I see the perfect one," he said, pointing toward a small booth. Inside was a painting of a beach with waves lapping at the shoreline and the sun beginning to set in the distance. Orange, red, and yellow streaks filled the sky.

"It is beautiful," she said as they got closer. "It's a little big, though, don't you think?" They were close enough now to see the size: 24 x 36. Then she read the title: "A Perfect Maui Sunset."

He noticed the title at the same time. "Look! It's a sign. This could have been painted at the very place we stayed." He asked the artist about the location. He described the beach, but couldn't recall the name. "It could be the same beach, hon."

"It might be," she smiled and admired it a moment longer. "Do you think it'll fit on the wall behind my couch?"

"Yeah, it'll look fine there."

She turned the painting around to see the price, and her eyes widened. Even if it was the same beach, the painting was more than she was prepared to spend.

But Andrew had already decided. "It's yours." He pulled out his credit card and handed it to the artist.

"No, I don't feel right about you paying for it. You just gave me an expensive gift last weekend." She protested. "I'll get it." She reached inside her purse for her credit card.

"I won't take no for an answer. I want to get this for you—for us. It'll be a wonderful reminder of our week in Maui—besides, the blues in the ocean will go perfectly with your other décor."

"So you're suddenly an interior decorator?" She smiled. "Never knew you to pay much attention to decorating before."

"Well, maybe I'm becoming more sensitive in a lot of areas." He grinned. "Whatever makes you happy," he said as the artist wrapped the painting in bubble wrap. "Anything else you want to look for while we're here?"

"Let's walk around the other side and see what's there—it's a gorgeous day."

After lunch at a Chinese restaurant, they headed back to the apartment. Andrew hung the painting for her, and they stood back to admire it.

"You were right," she said. "It does look great there, not too large at all. I love it. Thank you."

"Yep." He moved the couch back against the wall and picked up the tools. "Anything for my girl."

Shannon bristled inside a bit. *Am I his girl?*

"I'm going to imagine it's our beach," he said. "It sure does look like the same one. Hey, do you have any pictures we could compare it with? Oh wait, that's right . . . you got rid of everything." He shrugged. "Well, I'll see if I can find some when I get back. It is a beautiful painting."

Shannon nodded. "It is—it's exactly what the apartment needed. I didn't realize how empty the wall looked before. Want to take a walk around the lake before dinner?"

They returned to Shannon's apartment to watch a movie. Andrew kept kissing her, stroking her arm, her hair. She didn't resist at first, until he began implying that their relationship should be on a new level by now. She stood up to put some distance between them, and patiently restated her boundaries. Again. Andrew finally relented.

"Okay, but it's hard, Shan. How much longer are we just going to be dating? You know I want to get married."

So are the expensive gifts because he wants more than I'm giving him physically? I hope not, but it's starting to seem like it.

Their goodbye kiss that night was longer than usual, more passionate. But Shannon was determined not to weaken and get drawn into another level with him.

She pulled away and put a hand on his chest. "Good night, Andrew."

"You're killing me, you know."

"You'll survive."

"Okay, I'll be strong. Think about what you want to do next weekend," he said as he left.

She picked up the dessert dishes on the coffee table, then stepped back to admire the painting. It was beautiful. It took her thoughts straight back to the beach. She sank back onto the couch, and sadness overcame her. *What happened?* They'd been so much in love then, celebrating five years of marriage. *Yeah, and I thought we were still in love after ten years—but then everything changed.* Could it ever be the same? Had it ever been real for him? If it was, when did it change? When did he stop loving her? *He couldn't have loved me if he was having an affair; he chose to leave me.*

The lonely rejected feelings permeated her heart again, and she went to bed sad and depressed. About the only thing she did know was that she was tired of the rollercoaster.

Tuesday after work, Jen called to see if Shannon wanted to walk the dogs together. They spent a good half hour out on the trail before Jen asked the question Shannon had been dreading.

"So, what's happening with you and Andrew?"

Shannon stopped and faced her friend. Maybe dreading wasn't the right word. Maybe Jen could help her put some order to her thoughts.

"I thought I was doing okay, but then Max came in to talk to Rose and . . . Ugh, he's the reason I'm so confused. One minute I'm picturing myself with Andrew—I even asked to meet his daughter—and then the next minute, I'm drawn back to Max. It's driving me crazy."

The dogs kept moving. Jen gave a breathless laugh as she quickstepped to keep up. "Not to be funny, but . . . isn't it kind of exciting to have to decide between two such gorgeous guys?"

"Exciting isn't the word I would use." Shannon rolled her eyes, but she did allow a grin to pop out. "I'm thinking it's more like insane."

"Yeah," Jen said in a more somber tone. "This must be awfully hard for you. I've admired you for wanting to give your ex a second chance after everything that happened. I've asked myself what I would do—and I don't know how I'd react."

Shannon shrugged. "It's hard. I keep seeing little warning signs, but then—I guess it would be good to talk about it. Are you in a hurry to get back?"

"Not at all. Why don't we let the dogs play for a few minutes?"

"Thanks." Shannon breathed a sigh of relief.

"Sure. So what's going on?"

"First, he doesn't want to go to church, and I don't know what's up with that. We always went to church together. He could get here in time for the second service, but he's never interested. I usually go before he gets here."

"Maybe he's still feeling guilty about what he did?"

"Yeah, I thought about that. But if he's repentant, it seems like he would have dealt with the guilt and asked for forgiveness by now. And nobody here knows about all that. He's pretty evasive about spiritual things as a whole.

"And another red flag—Claire and her husband saw him at a restaurant with a woman. When I confronted him, he assured me it was a business meeting. I want to believe him, but . . . how do I know he's telling the truth?"

"That's a tough one because of his past record."

Shannon sighed, and they started walking again.

"And then—when I mentioned his daughter—he had the weirdest reaction. Almost like he was nervous talking about her. He doesn't have any pictures of her on his phone and he doesn't talk about her unless I bring her up. It bothered me, but I didn't realize why until I went to Claire's and watched her and Mark swoon over their baby. It's such a huge contrast to how he acts."

"Wow, I can understand why you're having doubts." Jen reached over and put a hand on Shannon's shoulder. "I'm sorry. I wish there were something I could do. I hope I didn't cause a problem by asking you about him."

"No, it's fine. Talking about it was good. All these thoughts have been swirling in my head. It's helped to speak them out. Some days I feel like such a mixed-up mess."

"Just trust God, Shannon. He won't let you down. Look how far He's brought you already—everything you've been through."

"That's what I keep telling myself." They stopped at the sidewalk between their two buildings. "Thanks for listening, Jen. It really helped."

❦

Andrew called on Thursday night. "What would you think about spending Sunday at a beach? I could come earlier so we can beat the crowds. It's supposed to be a good day and I know how much you love the beach."

"That sounds great. I've heard some coworkers raving about Pasture Beach, and I've been wanting to go. Could you bring some beach chairs? I don't have any here."

"Why don't you buy some and I'll reimburse you—you'll need them this summer."

"Okay, thanks. That's very thoughtful of you. I'll pick up some beach towels too, so I'll have them here."

"Sounds perfect. I'll plan to get there early, maybe around nine. Have a good night."

Shannon searched her closet unsuccessfully for her swimsuit. *Well, add a suit to the list—it's time for a new one anyway.* After work the next day, she found a bright blue suit, floral cover-up, and floppy sun hat. Sunday would be fun.

And then Claire called Saturday night.

"Shannon . . . I heard something today that surprised me. With all that's been going on with you and Andrew, I don't think he's told you everything."

"What do you mean?"

Claire hesitated, and her silence was disturbing. Whatever this was, it was big.

"Umm . . . I'm not sure, and maybe you do already know. I, uh, I heard that Sienna isn't his baby? I heard he hasn't been in her life for a couple of months."

"What?"

"But I heard it secondhand. I could be wrong. I just thought, with you saying how he doesn't show you pictures or anything, maybe I should tell you. Maybe that's why, and . . . I don't know why he'd lie about it though."

"Yeah, I don't either." They spoke for a few more minutes, then Claire hung up. Shannon went straight to her room and began praying. Andrew would be here early tomorrow morning. She would need God's help and wisdom to deal with this situation.

He greeted her with a hug, not the usual kiss, promptly at nine. She didn't mind. She smiled and invited him in but kept a physical distance between them. They were both quiet as they loaded the car and drove to the beach.

Pulling into the parking lot, he said, "We're in luck—a perfect spot." They unloaded their things and set up their space close to the water, knowing they would have to move back as the tide came in around noon. The air was still a bit chilly, but the weatherman was predicting warm sunshine for most of the day.

"This is nice. I needed this." She settled into her chair and dug her toes into the warm sand. "I've had a few stressful days at work—demanding clients, you know. I packed some coffee in the thermos, would you like some?"

"Sure, you think of everything."

"And, of course, Rose sent along some triple-berry scones."

"The best. She really could open a bakery—I wonder if she's ever thought about it." He paused to take a bite.

"I did ask her about it once, but she's happy with her shop and just a little bit of baking. It's a perfect set-up for her actually—her cottage, gardens, floral shop, and tea shop. She'd never find another place like it."

"True. But her pastries are the best. I occasionally pick up some scones in town, but they can't compare to hers. Did you ever ask her for the recipe?"

"I did, but they didn't come out like hers. I think I need a cast iron pan."

"Ahh, maybe a Christmas gift idea," he laughed.

Shannon gave him a sideways glance then turned her gaze to the water. *God, give me an opening,* she prayed. The sun felt good as she stretched out her legs and leaned back in her chair. She closed her eyes and let the heat soak into her body. She woke with a start some time later.

"Didn't take you long to relax," Andrew said with a laugh.

"Guess not—I didn't sleep well last night, and the sun gets me every time." She sat up, shaking her head. She really hadn't slept— she'd worried about the conversation they needed to have all night. But Andrew had no clue.

"I was sitting here, thinking about all the great times we've had at the beach," he said. "It's always been our favorite place to be together, hasn't it?"

"Mmm, yeah." Her voice trailed off. He gave her a funny look, and she decided it was time. "So, Andrew. Do you have any new pics of Sienna? I'd really like to see her."

"I told you, I don't like taking pictures."

"Well, what's she doing these days? Is she rolling over or crawling or . . . what? I'm not sure what stage she should be at."

"Umm . . . she's crawling. Let's go for a swim." He jumped up and reached down for her hand. She didn't move. "Shannon?"

"Sit down, Andrew. We need to talk."

He looked at her for a moment, then turned his chair to face hers and sat back down. "Why? What's wrong?"

She cleared her throat. "I heard some things yesterday, but I don't know if I believe them. About you and Sienna. I want you to tell me what's going on."

She watched as several emotions crossed his face. Concern, maybe fear. A momentary hardness. Then a muscle flexed in his jaw, and he gave her a contrite look.

"Oh. That. Uhh . . . Shan, I've been thinking a lot about the things you said about honesty and transparency." He took a deep breath. "I . . . I haven't been honest with you."

"Really." Her heart sank to her toes.

"Yeah, I know." He paused. "I was—this is hard," he stammered. "I was . . . *deceived* . . . by Lela."

"Lela! You're seeing her again?"

"No, no, I'm not. Just calm down and listen to me." He waved his hand, and she raised an eyebrow. Not that he noticed.

"Okay, I was stupid to think I could keep this from you, but I was afraid of losing you. I wanted to tell you several times, but I couldn't take the chance of ending our relationship."

"I'm listening."

"Three months after I started seeing her, she told me she was pregnant. That's why I left you, Shannon. I had to take responsibility for fathering a child. I thought it was the right thing to do. Turns out . . . Lela lied to me. Not long after Sienna was born, I found out—" He stopped and swallowed hard. "She isn't my daughter."

So what Claire had heard was correct. Shannon felt like she must be dreaming. She shielded her eyes from the sun to look straight into his. "What are you talking about?"

"I didn't know Lela was dating another man at the same time she was seeing me. He's the father, but he dumped her when she told him she was pregnant. She used me to get child support for Sienna. I've been the biggest fool in the world."

"I'd say."

"And I've hurt you and my parents—they love Sienna and now she's not in their lives anymore—or mine. It's been horrible. When you said you wanted to meet her, I didn't know what to say. I was still trying to find the right time to tell you."

"But you lied. You looked me straight in the face and told me you were being truthful, while you were lying. I don't know what to say now. I can't believe you would keep this from me." She didn't know whether to cry or throw something at him. "So how did you find out?"

"The real father had a change of heart and wanted to be back in Lela's life and take responsibility for Sienna. Lela was getting support money from both of us for a while, until she finally decided to tell me the truth. I thought about taking her to court to recoup the child support, but I decided to let it go, for Sienna's sake. Don't you see? I was conned."

"Conned." Shannon's laugh was more disdainful than amused. "You aren't the victim here—Sienna is."

"I know, I know. I worry about how she's adjusting." He looked sad.

"Well, it's not like you were there every day anyway . . . or so you said. I don't know how you could let me go on thinking you were still parenting on Saturdays and Wednesdays—and lying about you and your parents spending time with her." She began stuffing her things into her duffel bag.

"I'm sorry I didn't tell you the truth—I felt so trapped, and then . . . one lie led to another because I didn't know how to handle it."

"Is this why you wanted to get married right away? So when I found out the truth it would be too late? And the necklace . . . and the painting?" She felt like she was going to throw up. "What else are you lying to me about?"

"I'm not. I wanted to get married as soon as we started dating again—you have to believe me. I want our old life back. When I say you're the best thing that happened to me, I mean it. You have such a pure heart. You're a good person, with wonderful qualities—you're not like any other woman I've dated." He reached toward her hand.

She pulled away. "I don't know what to believe anymore. Why did you come to work that day? Is that the day Lela dumped you? I thought you were going to marry her."

He sighed impatiently. "I was willing to get married because of Sienna, but Lela said she wasn't ready. I think she was hoping all along the other guy would come back. But I couldn't get you out of my mind and I wanted to see you—to see if we had a chance together. Come on, Shannon. You know we can be good together."

That was the last straw. She jumped up and added her folded towel to her bag. "My stomach's in knots," she said. "I want to go home."

He collected their belongings and stomped all the way to the car, kicking up sand. She followed, her heart in her throat.

He popped the trunk and they dropped their stuff inside. Then he moved around her to open her door. She slid in without a word.

He looked worried as he leaned in to see her face. "Shannon, I was wrong not to tell you sooner. I wanted to, but every time I thought about bringing it up, I knew it would ruin what we had."

"And look what happened," she said dryly. "Ruined is the right word, isn't it?" She pulled her door shut.

It was a long, cold, silent ride back to her apartment.

He carried the chairs and cooler up to her apartment, where she made it clear he wasn't coming in. She stood in the doorway facing him. "You can set that right here outside the door." A hand went to her hip. She was trying to be calm, but she was fighting fury and tears. Neither of which she would let him see. "I've been listening to you all morning, Andrew. You've used the words *conned, deceived, lied to* . . . Well, those words describe how I'm feeling right now. I need space. I don't want to see you next weekend. I can't. This is a lot to process—on top of what I've already tried to work through."

He put his hand on her arm. "I never wanted to hurt you. I love you. I didn't know how to tell you. I was trying to protect *us.*" She shook him off and stepped inside.

"I'm not sure there is an *us* anymore." She tried to push the door shut, but he placed his foot in the doorway. "Honestly, I think you were trying to protect yourself."

"Shannon. Don't—" His voice was strident, loud. Her eyes widened, and he stopped. He was quieter, pleading when he began again. "Honey, please don't give up on me. On us. You know everything now—everything. I love you . . . and I thought you loved me. We can survive this. Together, I know we can."

"Just go. I'm tired. I don't want to talk about any of this anymore today." She pushed harder on the door.

"Okay. But when can I call you?"

"I don't know. I need space." He moved his foot, and she slammed the door.

She waited till she saw his car drive away, then she gathered the chairs and cooler from the hallway. She put the food away and tossed the towels in the laundry, then wandered into the living room. Finally, she stopped in front of the couch, staring at the painting, frozen in thought, and crying. The seascape suddenly became a painful reminder of the fantasy world she had created, a stark contrast to reality. Instead of serenity and peace, she felt only anger and tension.

She was as alone and lonely as she had been on the night he'd left. She had wasted months with him—believing him, forgiving him, hoping for a restored relationship. Now she felt utterly used, deceived. The words she'd started to believe again—I love you— rang in her head, cruel and tortuous echoes. *I let my guard down, and he took advantage of me . . . again. He thinks only about himself. I will never trust him again. Not now.*

She cried out to God in tears, picked up her journal, and began pouring out words on the pages until she was tired and deplete of emotions. If only she could go to sleep and wake up without the lump in her throat and ache in her heart. But sleep was not to come—too many thoughts. Her parents had been right—he hadn't changed. In some ways he was worse, and that made the pain more unbearable. She felt embarrassed and ashamed. *How am I going to tell them and everyone else? He's made a fool out of me—again.*

She took a personal day on Monday—several people in the office had known she was going to the beach with him, and she didn't feel like trying to fake her feelings or having a public meltdown. She quickly found that sitting still, however, opened the door to too many thoughts, so she busied herself with laundry, housework, and a quick trip to the grocery store. About four-thirty, Jen called to say she was going to Rose's and asked if she would like to come along.

"Sure, I didn't go to work today. It'll be good to get out with you."

Shannon knew she hadn't managed to conceal the dark circles under her eyes, but she almost laughed as Jen stepped back in surprise when she opened her door.

"You sure you're up to going? I can go tomorrow night if you'd rather just talk. Are you okay?"

"I'm okay. I need to get out—these walls are closing in on me. We can talk at the Cozy."

Jen drove, and Shannon took the time to relax as best she could. She wasn't prepared for the rush of emotion, however, that hit her as they entered the Amaryllis and Rose's expressive eyes took in her appearance.

"What a nice surprise to see you two this evening," Rose said.

"Hi, Rose," Jen replied. "I'm looking for a birthday gift for a friend." As the two discussed what Jen was looking for, Shannon made her way to a corner table in the Tea Cozy. She sat down facing the wall and worked to compose herself again.

Jen completed her purchase, then joined her at the table. "Things aren't good, are they?"

"That's an understatement. This morning I wanted to pull the covers over my head and stay there—didn't want to face the world."

"I'm sorry. Andrew again?"

"Who else. Just when I thought he couldn't do anything more

hurtful, he proved me wrong." She explained their conversation at the beach. "He's such a jerk."

Jennifer's eyes were wide. "I don't know what to say, I really don't. I'm so sorry, Shannon." She reached across the table to touch her hand. "But, yeah, I'd say he's a real jerk right now."

Shannon shook her head. Her voice was hushed as she said, "It's over. I won't see him anymore—I can't. He destroyed the progress we made, well—the progress I thought we'd made. I can't figure out why he would lie to me about Sienna for so long. Nothing makes sense. And if I hadn't found out—when would he have told me?" Her eyes revealed the depth of hurt. "I don't think I could believe anything he says anymore."

"Did he say why he didn't tell you sooner?" Jen looked puzzled.

She shrugged. "He had a lot of excuses—mostly because he thought it would end our relationship. But for the life of me, I don't understand how he could think lying and delaying would end well, at the same time he was telling me how truthful he was being." The anger welled up inside again. "I really believe the reason he wanted to get married right away was so when he did tell me the truth—or when I found out—it would be too late. He was sure I wouldn't divorce him over that. He denied it, of course, but it's the only thing that makes sense."

"Yeah, that's hard to understand. I guess all those doubts were there for a reason. Intuitively, you knew something was wrong." Her cell phone rang but she sent it to voicemail. "Kevin . . . I'll call him back later."

"I'm really happy for you, Jen—you got a great guy." Shannon wiped her eyes with a napkin.

"Thanks. But I had to date a few losers before I found him." Jen smiled.

"Yeah, but I was married to one." She managed a half-smile. "Guess I'm a glutton for punishment—or the most gullible person in the world. Or both."

"You did what you thought was right by giving him a second

chance, Shannon. Don't fault yourself—ever. It was the admirable thing to do. But I'm so sorry he hurt you again." She stood up. "Care for some more tea?"

"Sure. Thanks."

Jen brought some cookies and the tea to the table just as Rose walked over. "Shannon, I was wondering if your amaryllis bulb has any shoots yet."

"Nothing yet—it still looks pretty dead." She was trying to project confidence, but knew Rose could see through the façade.

"Oh, it will start growing again, soon. Don't give up, dear." She patted Shannon's shoulder and gave her a knowing look—like, *I see your pain.*

"I remember what you told me about the journey of the amaryllis, and it does give me hope." She sighed. "And that's what I need right now." She didn't want to fake her feelings anymore.

"I sensed that, dear. Let me know if I can be of any help, anytime. My door is always open." She smiled as she returned to the floral shop.

"She doesn't miss anything, does she?" Shannon said. "It's like she has a sixth sense about people."

"Yes, she does—it's a gift she has. And many have benefited from her gift. I've seen a lot of hurting people come through her door, and she has a way of encouraging each one—either through the imperfect items that she creatively makes perfect again, or the kind words she shares from her heart. People know she really cares."

"She's one of the most compassionate people I've ever met—it's why I keep volunteering here. I hope some of it will rub off on me."

"Well, you're pretty compassionate too—which is why you were willing to give Andrew a second chance. Even when he didn't deserve it."

She was able to smile a little and it felt good—a fleeting moment free of anger and disappointment. "Thanks for listening, Jen. You're a good friend—and I needed one tonight. I'm dreading telling my folks. They never did think it would work. I should have listened to them. Would have saved a lot of heartache."

"You didn't have any way of knowing for sure how things would work out and you were willing to try—all to your credit."

"Thanks. We probably better head back."

"Does this mean you might renew things with Max?" Jen said in the car.

"I don't know. I don't want him to think he's second best . . . or an afterthought because it didn't work out with Andrew."

"Whatever you decide—it will get better each day, I'm sure."

"I hope so—it certainly can't get any worse." They both chuckled. Then Shannon shuddered as she remembered saying that once before—and things got much worse.

Chapter Nineteen 🌹

Tuesday after work, Shannon drove home through a rainstorm. Leaving her car, she grabbed the mail quickly and darted into her apartment. She closed the door and tossed the mail on the kitchen table. It wasn't until later, while she was preparing dinner, that she glanced at the stack of mail again. She picked up the top envelope and groaned as she recognized the familiar handwriting sprawled across it. *Oh, great.* She sat down and opened the envelope, pulled out the letter and laid it on the table, then apprehensively began to read.

> Dear Shannon,
>
> You told me not to call so I'm respecting you. But I'm miserable not knowing how you are and what you're thinking. I know I sound like a broken record, but I'm sorry. You have to believe me. I love you, and I'm devastated because I messed things up again. I hope you'll give me some credit for telling you the truth—even if I did make a huge mistake in the timing. I'm not as

intuitive as you are. I let my fear of losing you outweigh my responsibility to be honest. I know that's not an excuse, and I know I hurt you again. I can't imagine my life without you. I had so many plans for us. I have no future without you. Give me another chance to make it up to you. You're a very caring and compassionate person, and I hope you'll find compassion in your heart for me. I would give anything to be able to go back in time and restore the love we had. I know we could be happy again. Don't shut me out of your life.

Love always, Andrew.

She pushed the letter aside, finished her dinner, cleaned up the dishes, opened the rest of the mail, and paid some bills. Then she refolded the letter, placed it back in the envelope, and called her parents. It was time to let them know what was going on. They listened quietly as she relayed the sudden twist of events. They were too kind and gracious to say "I told you so."

"Shannon, we're here to support you in whatever decision you make for your future," Dad said. "It's your life, and only you can make these difficult decisions for what's best for you."

"And that poor little girl." Mom chimed in. "Are you okay? I'm sorry you've had such a shock—I can imagine it's very hurtful. Thank you for letting us know what's going on. We hadn't heard from you for a while, so we were wondering if things were okay."

"I'm fine. I didn't call sooner, because . . . honestly, I'm embarrassed to be in this situation."

"Honey, there's nothing for you to be embarrassed about. You were hopeful you two could have a future together," Dad said calmly.

"I told him I didn't want to see him again—I can't trust him. It's over and I'm going to let him know I'm serious about ending it."

"Okay, sunshine. You know we are always in your corner. Love you."

"Thanks, Dad."

"And you know we will be praying—as we always do. Take care of yourself—I'm sure this has all been quite stressful," Mom added.

"Yeah, it's been the pits, but I think things will get better now. Well, I need to get some things done. Talk to you again soon."

"Bye," they both said.

The next morning as she was packing her lunch, she glanced at the amaryllis bulb on the table—a small green shoot was emerging. *Hope.* She held the pot up to the sunlight near the slider for a better look at the baby leaf that had pushed through the dried remains of previous shoots. *You're not dead; you still have some life left in you.*

All day she felt unsettled at work, she couldn't shake an overriding sense that the sooner she responded to the letter, the better. She couldn't let it linger in her thoughts and create more stress. If she was going to move on, she had to make sure Andrew understood clearly that his future didn't include her. It hurt because she did have feelings for him, and she might never know what was real—for either of them.

After dinner and a long walk with Willow to collect her thoughts, she sat at the table and began her response to the letter. Two grueling attempts later, the letter was finished—a much shorter version than the first two.

> Andrew, I read your letter. I think we've already said everything that needs to be said, so I'm asking you not to write or call again. We need to move on with our lives. Separately. I can no longer keep the necklace, so I'll be returning it via certified mail this weekend. I wish you well in the future. Shannon

Done. She felt queasy, filled with the same anxiety she'd felt as she'd signed the divorce papers. This time, somehow, felt worse.

It felt like signing a death certificate because hope had died. She poured herself some tea in her grandmother's cup and moved to the porch, where she reflected back to the day she'd almost died.

How could she have given him the power to make her so despondent? How could she have been that weak to have wanted to give up on life? Never again. Now she would persevere and be even stronger. She'd learned a lot about herself by moving away, starting a new job, making a new life—yes. She had a new life, and it wasn't going to include him anymore. The uneasiness gradually left. She felt empowered—she was making the choice that was right for her.

Back inside, she folded the letter and slipped it into an envelope. With a firm hand, she addressed it, sealed it, and as an act of finality, added the stamp. Then she went to her room and opened her jewelry box. She took out the necklace and placed it in its original box. She looked at it carefully, counted the jewels again. She wasn't surprised that they seemed to have lost their shine. When Andrew had fastened the chain around her neck, she'd seen it as a sparkling symbol of his love, but now it represented only manipulation and deceit. She closed the box and taped it shut. Then she brushed her hands together—*done and done!*

She slept better that night than she had in weeks.

"Good morning, Rose." Shannon greeted her friend in the doorway on Saturday morning. "Guess what—my amaryllis is starting to grow."

"Wonderful. You'll see growth every day now."

Shannon put on her apron and leaned in toward Rose at the counter. "It's over with Andrew," she whispered. "I'll fill you in later."

"Are you okay?" Rose looked concerned.

"Actually, yes . . . better than I thought. Once I made my decision, it was easier. You know, the uncertainty was driving me crazy. But it's final now, so I can move on."

Rose gave her a quick hug. "We'll talk later," she said.

The morning passed as Shannon and Madelaine waited on customers. Rose stayed in the back, making her creative repairs on several containers. Customers came and went, the little bell over the door jingling at each entry and exit.

The peaceful morning was interrupted when the bell over the door clanged, and an angry voice rang out.

"We have to talk. Now."

Shannon froze, nearly dropping the vase she was wrapping for a customer.

"No, Andrew. You need to leave. I'm working—and I have nothing more to say to you."

"Yes, you do." His voice was loud enough to bring Rose bustling out of the back room. "I need an explanation. You can't just cut me off like that."

"Sir, Shannon is correct, this is not the right place for you to talk to her." Rose's voice was firm. "I would like you to leave now."

"Hell, no! This is the only place where I know I can talk to her, and I'm going to talk to her." His face was glowing red; one hand formed a tight fist.

Shannon was beginning to quake inside—she had never seen him like this before. "Andrew, please leave. You're making a scene."

"I don't care," he growled. "I have to see you." He stumbled as he moved closer to her. "You can't write me off. I was your husband—how can that not matter anymore?"

Rose stepped aside and quietly called the police. Returning, she joined Shannon behind the counter and took hold of her hand.

"Andrew, have you been drinking?" Shannon asked.

Rose turned to her, shaking her head. "Hush, child," she said. Customers had begun to gather, watching and listening intently. In a firm voice, she instructed, "Madelaine, please take our customers to the tea shop for some refreshments. I'll be there shortly."

Andrew moved closer to the counter, his stare fixed on Shannon.

"The police have been called," Rose stated. "If you are still here when they arrive, you will be arrested. I suggest you leave quietly now."

Andrew sneered. "How many police do you have in this Podunk town anyway? I'll leave when I'm ready."

"He must be drunk," Shannon whispered to Rose. "I've never seen him like this."

"It's okay. You stay back here behind the counter." She pulled Shannon closer.

Soon one police officer entered through the front door and another entered through the back slider. "What's going on, sir?" the officer asked Andrew.

"I'm just trying to talk to my ex-wife—is that against the law?" He was beginning to slur his words.

"Let's take it outside. You're upsetting the customers." He motioned toward the door as the officer in back moved in.

"Then she needs to come outside too, so we can talk." He looked back at Shannon. "Are you coming?"

"No, sir, she's not. You and I are going to talk. Alone." The officer slowly approached Andrew, who pushed him away with a hard shove and a string of profanities. The officer in back ran forward, grabbed Andrew from behind, and clamped on the handcuffs. He became unruly and shouted more profanities as the officers walked him out to the patrol car. Finally, one drove away, and the other officer returned to the shop to take the names of those who were there.

Shannon watched the car speed away, siren blaring. She put her head on Rose's shoulder and moaned. "This is a nightmare—I'm so humiliated. I don't even know him right now."

"I know, dear. It'll be okay. I'll be right back after I talk to the customers. You stay right here." Rose squeezed her hand before she left for the tea shop.

She and the officer returned to the counter together. Rose introduced him.

"Officer Garonna, this is Shannon Enright. She volunteers at the shop on Saturdays."

He reached out his hand. "Pleased to meet you, Shannon. I'm sorry it was under these circumstances." Turning to Rose, he asked, "Could the three of us go to the cottage for your statements?"

"Of course. Madelaine can cover for us." With a quick instruction, she led the way through the gardens.

Officer Garonna took out his iPad, a notebook, and some forms. Rose recounted Andrew's actions, words, tone, and mannerisms. The officer asked if she had felt threatened.

"No, but I was concerned for Shannon. He was demanding and getting forceful, insisting that Shannon talk to him, right then and there."

"Thank you, Rose. Shannon, would you describe the incident in your words?"

The reality of the moment hit her, and Shannon started to shake. A police officer was taking her statement about her ex-husband. She shuddered. "I'm sorry, I'm having a hard time taking all this in." Trying to stay composed, she began describing what had happened as best she could recall.

"What was he pressing you to talk to him about?"

"We'd begun dating again, after the divorce. Everything was going along well, and then I found out about something that he had been keeping from me, several things, really. Significant things." She looked at Rose. "I haven't told you any of this yet.

"Anyway, it was a game-changer for me, and I broke off our relationship this week. I never dreamed he would show up here. I thought since it was over, we would both move on."

The officer looked up from his notes, "Apparently, he thought otherwise. Does he have a history of drinking or abusive behavior?"

"No, never abusive behavior. When we were married, he'd have a few beers or wine occasionally, but I've never seen him like that before. Do you mind if I stand up? I'm pretty nervous. Walking around might help."

"Of course not. Go ahead. I hope I'm not making you nervous." He smiled. "I'm pretty easy to talk to, right, Rose?"

"Yes, you are."

Shannon walked to the front door, looked out the large window briefly, then came back to her chair. "No—it's the whole situation." She took a deep breath. "Just recalling what happened . . . and I keep seeing his eyes. They weren't normal, they were very dark. I never saw that angry look before—it was really unsettling, hard to describe." She began to weep.

"Take your time. You're doing fine at describing, Shannon. Did you feel threatened? Do you feel safe?"

"What do you mean?" She was shocked at his question. "He would never harm me. He's just upset and didn't handle the situation well—that's all."

"We can't make that assumption. It's my job is to make sure you are safe. You have the option of filing a restraining order."

"A restraining order? Oh, heavens no! That's not necessary. He's not harmful. I know him too well—he would never hurt me. I doubt he'll bother me again." She was becoming more uncomfortable with the questions and the implication that she was in some kind of danger.

"Shannon," Rose said. "I know you can't imagine Andrew trying to harm you, but I have worked with several women who thought the same thing and, unfortunately, were proven wrong." She looked at the officer and then at Shannon. "It's a protective measure for you that sends a strong message to him. It makes it clear there will be serious consequences if he bothers you again. You don't have to decide now, but please think about it—it could give you peace of mind, and me too. I can help you with the paperwork."

"Yes," Officer Garonna said. "Rose could be a great help if you decide to file."

"This is all too much to take in. I'm feeling very tired. Is there anything else you need from me?" She closed her eyes, took a deep breath, and tried to control her tears.

"No, I have enough for now." He stood up and shook Shannon's hand. "Thank you for talking with me. We want to keep you safe."

"I know—I hope I haven't been rude or disrespectful. I've never been in this situation before. It's overwhelming," she managed a half-smile.

"I understand. We're here to help. If you hear from him in a threatening or alarming way or if he shows up again uninvited, give me a call immediately." He handed her his card.

"Thank you. I will."

"It was nice to meet you, Shannon. And it's always nice to see you, Rose."

They watched him as he walked back to the shop, then Rose put her arm around Shannon.

"I'm so sorry you were traumatized today, dear," she said. "You stay here as long as you'd like. I won't need you the rest of the day, but if you aren't ready to go back to your apartment, you just feel free to stay here in the cottage."

"Thank you, Rose." Shannon's voice was small. "I think I'll sit in the gardens for a while."

Chapter Twenty

"Lord, I can't believe this is happening." Shannon sat on the bench in the garden, praying. "Did the alcohol make him so angry? I was afraid. I've never seen him act like that. Why is this happening? I prayed for clarity. How could I have been so blind? I don't think I really know him. I need Your help. Amen." The tears came again, grief pouring out from the depths of her lonely soul. She walked slowly around the gardens, seeking peace to calm her broken heart . . . but there was none to be found. The piercing pain inside could not be soothed.

Rose joined her and placed an arm around her as they walked. "My dear, let the tears come—they are healing tears." They sat down together on the bench. Shannon held her face in her hands and sobbed. Rose gently patted her back as they sat in silence.

A cool breeze blew, and she looked up into the warm sun. Its rays brought her a gentle reassurance. Life goes on, there would be a new day tomorrow, and she would get through this. God had strengthened her before; she would trust Him again. The words filtered through her mind. She knew they were truth, but they just felt like platitudes right now.

After a while, Rose asked, "How's your amaryllis doing?"

"Growing. The green stalk is getting taller." She sniffled.

"And so shall you, my dear. You can trust in the Lord. You've had a shock and a great disappointment. I'm sorry you've been hurt again, but the truth is, we learn to trust Him more through suffering. I am convinced that God uses our pain to help others. One day, this experience will allow you to help another to bear her burden."

Shannon sniffed again, then reached out to the older woman with a hug. "You are such a wonderful friend and mentor. You always offer encouragement, godly advice, and empathy. Thank you."

"It's my pleasure, Shannon. I'm so glad God brought you to the Amaryllis. You have a very gentle spirit, and I know God will be faithful to guide you. He's still in the healing business, you know." She smiled.

"I know, and I'm grateful for all He's done in my life already. When I was married and things were going so well, I didn't feel like I needed God anymore. I guess I became prideful and tried to handle everything on my own." She looked up toward the sun again and continued. "Then, during the divorce, I became angry at God for letting it happen. It seemed unfair. I got so depressed I didn't want to live anymore. I'll never get to that place again, though, because I know no matter what happens, there's always hope—in tomorrow."

"Yes, there is. And I'm thankful God kept you safe."

"Yes, He did, miraculously." She cringed, recalling that awful day. "I'm thankful He brought me here to Loughton Valley, too, where I have new friends and a good job. And being here meant meeting you and helping at the Amaryllis. I really am blessed."

"It's so nice to see you smile again. God has more good plans for you in the future too."

Shannon nodded. "I know that in my heart," she said. "My head just needs to catch up."

"That's true for all of us, my dear."

"Thanks. I think I'll head back to my apartment." They walked back to the shop, where Madelaine was waiting.

"Shannon," she said, her face alight with compassion. "Is there anything I can do to help?"

"No, I'm okay. But thanks for asking, Madelaine." She picked up her purse from the cubby behind the counter and walked to the back slider. "I'm heading home. I'll be okay. I'll see you both next Saturday." Then she stepped out into the late afternoon to get in her car.

She was almost there when a car door opened, and she turned to see who it was.

"Andrew!" She hadn't noticed his car in the lot not far from hers. "What are you doing here?"

"Calm down, Shan. I just want to talk. I know . . . I overreacted. I'm sorry."

"I don't want to talk to you—I told you we have nothing more to talk about." She unlocked her car, opened the door, and got in. Andrew quickly slid in on the passenger side.

"Get out, Andrew. You're making me very uncomfortable." She gripped the steering wheel tightly, trying to stay calm. She looked straight ahead, focusing on the building next door. She didn't want to look at him. He smelled of alcohol.

"I thought you told me how wonderful Rose was." His voice was rough. "Yeah, she's so wonderful, she called the cops on me."

"How'd you get out so soon?"

"I paid the fine. They didn't have anything on me. But you didn't stop it—you could have told them everything was okay, but you didn't. Now I have a court date."

"And you're blaming me? Unbelievable." She turned toward

him, alarmed to see how red his face was getting. "I'm asking you to get out of my car—I don't want to talk to you." She pulled her phone out of her purse. He caught her intent and shifted gears quickly.

"Okay, sorry. You don't need to call anyone. You're right—it wasn't your fault. But I wanted to talk." His voice took on a whining tone. "I needed to hear from you face-to-face why you're pushing me out of your life. I have to know why, Shannon. I thought you loved me."

"You know why, Andrew."

"Because I took extra time before I told you about Sienna? You're not being fair. I told you, I was blindsided. I didn't know how to tell you. Okay, so I handled it wrong, but—I was thinking of you. I didn't want to hurt *you*. So why are you trying to end our relationship? We've been through worse together. I thought we were working through everything."

"If you really don't understand, then there's nothing more I can say to explain it to you." She opened her door, got out, and walked back to the shop. She opened the door and stepped inside. He followed.

When Rose saw him, she stalked toward them. "Everything okay, Shannon?"

"Yes. Andrew is leaving." She turned toward him. "Aren't you?"

"Sure, I'll leave. I don't want your *friend* to call the cops on me again. But we are going to talk, Shannon. You owe it to me." He walked back toward his car as Shannon watched through the slider to make sure he had left.

"Let's go next door and have some tea." Rose caught Shannon's hand and coaxed her through the doorway.

Thoughts were swirling. *Why can't he leave me alone? What does he want from me?* Her hands were shaking as she placed them on the table.

Rose touched her hand gently. "Are you okay?"

"No," she cried. "He doesn't get it!"

"I think it's a good idea to write down the things he said to you, while they're fresh in your mind. We may need to call Officer Garonna again. Andrew seems determined to keep contacting you." Rose looked concerned.

"Well, he reeked of alcohol when he got in my car. Guess he left the police department and stopped at another bar." She took a sip of tea. "I'll jot things down, but I don't think I need to call the police again."

"Shannon, he behaved in a verbally abusive way earlier today and it's concerning. Officer Garonna was alluding to it also. Someone who is abusive is also controlling, so he may not let things go. We want you to be safe."

Shannon shrugged her shoulders. "I know—but it's so surreal. One day I'm thinking we're going to get married again, and the next, he's handcuffed in the back of a police car. I can't sort it all out in my mind." She picked up her purse. "I'm going to try going home again. Thanks for everything, Rose."

Even with Rose watching, she was a bit apprehensive walking back to her car. She knew she was overreacting—she'd watched him leave—but she just didn't feel safe. She drove home, watching her rearview mirror. At the same time, she replayed his actions and words, both from the shop and in her car. Maybe it would be a good idea to write some things down.

At the apartment, she described what had happened and what he'd said as she remembered it. But what she couldn't completely describe was his anger—she simply didn't know where it was coming from or why she'd never seen it before. Would it go away, or was she really in danger?

The beachscape on the wall caught her attention again, and she knew it had to go. Placing it by the door, she put the leash on Willow, then carried the picture to her car. She'd drop it off at the consignment shop after work. She led Willow on a short walk, intending to make some dinner when she got back. Instead, she sat down on the couch and, before she knew it, she was sound asleep.

When she got home Monday after work, she found a hand-written note in her mailbox. The handwriting was unmistakable. She read it on the way back to her apartment.

"Shan, I'm not letting this go—I'm not letting you go. We belong together. We were making it work and it was beautiful—just like it was before. We were happy. I know you were happy too—you can't deny it. I need you in my life. We have to talk. Any place you want. I can't live without you. Andrew."

He's crazy. She folded the note and placed it in the notebook where she'd recorded the events at the Amaryllis. *He'll get the message soon enough if I ignore him.*

She assumed he'd placed the note in her box on Saturday after she watched him leave the Amaryllis, but—*What if he was here again on Sunday?* That was a concerning thought. *Surely not.*

"He'll get over it," she said aloud. "I'm gonna ignore his note. He'll figure it out if I don't respond. The sooner he gets over it, the better."

Saturday came around again, and Shannon, unable to sleep, got to the shop a little early. "Morning, Rose."

"Good morning," Rose said with a big smile. "We have a large order today, so I'm glad you're here early. There's a ladies' luncheon at a local church and we're making the centerpieces. No specific instructions . . . just ten floral arrangements for the tables. I have extra flowers in the cooler—Madelaine's in there now. Are you doing okay today?"

"I'm fine—busy week at work kept my mind occupied." She put on her apron and joined Madelaine in the cooler.

"Hey, Shannon. I've been thinking about you. I'm sure sorry about your ex. How are you holding up?"

"He made quite a scene here didn't he?" She felt embarrassed again. "It's pretty bizarre—the whole thing. But I'm moving on. Thanks for asking. So, how can I help?"

"We're going with pink and rose tones with white accents. Rose ordered a lot of variety to choose from. We can each make five bouquets."

They selected the flowers while Rose took ten embellished containers from the shelves in the shop. Madelaine said, "Hey, while we're still in the cooler, I wanted to mention something. Yesterday the chief of police came to the shop, and he and Rose went to the cottage. They were there for quite a while. I assumed it was related to what happened with your ex, but when I asked her, she said it wasn't. I could tell she'd been crying. I wonder what that was about."

"Oh, very strange, I have no idea. I hope it wasn't anything serious." Shannon replied.

"Yeah, me too."

After the arrangements were completed and placed on the counter, Shannon stood back and admired them. "They are lovely. Are they being picked up, or do we need to deliver them?"

"They're sending a van over, so we need to pack them in the boxes behind the counter. Someone should be here in thirty minutes. Thanks, girls—great job."

Shannon and Madelaine padded the boxes, placed the containers carefully inside, and helped load them in the van when it arrived. They spent the rest of the morning waiting on customers, restocking cards, and refilling refreshments in the Tea Cozy. Shannon glanced at the clock and was surprised at the time.

"Jen is meeting me here, and we're going out for lunch at eleven. I think I'll freshen up before she gets here," she said, then walked to the ladies' room in the back. As she made her way back to the front counter, Jen and Max walked through the front door together.

"Look who I found outside," Jen said.

"Hi, Shannon." Max's whole face lit up in a big smile.

"Hi, Max. It's good to see you again." *Why do I feel so giddy when I see him?*

"Turns out we're both here to see you." Jen grabbed Shannon in a quick hug. "You and I can get together another time. I was coming here anyway—I need to pick up a housewarming gift." Shannon started to protest, but Jen just smiled. "Nope—it's all good."

"I really don't want to change your plans," Max said. "I could come back after you two go to lunch."

"No worries. We can reschedule, right, Shannon?"

It didn't really sound like she had a choice. Not that she minded terribly. "Okay, sure. Thank you for being flexible," she called as Jen walked over to the gift section.

Max came closer. "Would you like to go to lunch?"

"Yes, I would. Thank you." They walked to his car, and he opened the door for her. She wasn't sure why she was feeling nervous being in his car again—but this was a good nervous.

"Where would you like to go?"

"How about the barbecue place? I know you like it there, and I haven't been for a while."

"Perfect. You look lovely, by the way. I've missed you." He turned his head toward her and smiled.

"Thank you. I've . . . missed you too." She wondered if he knew about Andrew. *Of course he does. He knows everyone in town—the officer probably told him.*

After they were seated and ordered, Max leaned in toward her at the table. "Shannon, I don't want to make you uncomfortable, but I know what happened last weekend," he said in a hushed tone. "You don't have to talk about it if you don't want to, but I'm assuming it's over with him?"

"As over as it can be. So, how'd you find out? I suppose it's all over town since there were customers in the store when he showed up."

"I know you don't take the newspaper, but we do print the arrests. I talked to Officer Garonna. I'm really sorry—it must have been traumatic for you."

"Yeah, that's a good way to describe it. Well, I'm glad you know."

"Has he bothered you again?"

"Once. But I made it clear it's over, and we don't have any unfinished business."

"You need to promise you'll contact me or Officer Garonna if he bothers you again. I heard he got aggressive, and that worries me. Promise?"

"I promise. But I doubt I'll hear from him again." She waved a hand. "Enough about him. What's new in your life?"

The waitress brought the food. Max offered a quick prayer, and they dug in.

"I forgot how great their food is," Shannon said as she savored her first bite of the barbecued pulled pork.

"I know—it's the best for miles around. Great choice for lunch." He winked. "Not much exciting news in my life. All the articles about the town center's shop owners are finished, so it's mostly sports now. How's your job going?"

"The same."

Max put his fork down. "Shannon, I really wanted to talk today to see if we could date again—when you're ready, of course. I don't want to pressure you, but I want you to know how much I've missed you and would love for us to be a couple again." His blue eyes beamed.

"I would like that too, Max." She smiled back longingly. They chatted as if they had never been apart, and spent some time catching up on each other's lives. Shannon felt comfortable with him, as always, and realized she'd never felt this comfortable with Andrew.

"Would you like to take a stroll around the town center—where we had our first date?" Max asked as he signed the bill.

"That sounds like fun." She laughed. "First date . . . that seems like a long time ago now, doesn't it?"

"Too long. But I'm thankful I'm with you now." They walked to the car and he drove to a parking spot near the gazebo. He held the door as she got out of the car, then they walked hand in hand to the bench.

"You know, after our first date, Jen called me as soon as I got home because she'd seen us sitting here. She gave me the third degree."

"How funny. One of my coworkers saw us also and wanted to know who the gorgeous woman was. He's single and said if he'd seen you first, he would have asked you out. I told him hands off." He held her hand tighter.

"Oh, the woes of a small town." They both laughed, then she sighed. "I really do love it here. I'm glad I moved to little old Loughton Valley."

"Not nearly as happy about it as I am." He put his arm around her in a gentle hug. When their eyes met, she melted into his, remembering their first kiss. She felt safe and peaceful with him by her side—a secure feeling she had missed. They talked for another thirty minutes, recalling some of their dates.

"I'm not ready to take you back," Max finally said. "Do you have plans for the rest of the day?"

"No, but I will need to let Willow out in a few hours."

"How's she doing?"

"She's great. I'm so glad I have her—she's a perfect companion. It's true that animals have a sixth sense. She stays even closer to me when I'm upset . . . which lately has been often, unfortunately."

Max turned to face her. "I feel terrible about what you've been through, and also helpless because I wasn't able to be there for you."

He shook his head. "I'm really angry about the pain he caused too."

She shrugged. "There wasn't anything anyone could do—I just had to walk through it. I didn't see the signs along the way telling me something wasn't right. Well, I saw some of them, but I didn't put it all together. Guess I was pretty naïve."

"Because you're such a good person—you only see the best in people. You're one of the most caring people I know." He squeezed her shoulder gently, leaned over, and kissed her cheek.

Their eyes met again—words weren't needed. In the moment, they both knew they were in love. A solitary tear seeped out from her eye—Max wiped it away softly, still gazing into her bright green eyes. "I didn't mean to make you cry."

"A happy tear, and I'm glad you did." She laid her head on his shoulder. They sat quietly for a few more minutes, enjoying the closeness.

"Since we have the rest of the day, what would you like to do?" he asked.

"Let's swing by the apartment to let Willow out, and then, if you don't mind, I'd like to go to the outdoor mall. I'm looking for a framed picture for my living room and there's a great art gallery there." They walked hand in hand back to his car.

Willow met them at the door of the apartment, tail wagging. Max bent down and scratched her back. "Hey, girl! How've you been?" Her ecstatic response was more confirmation for Shannon.

"You know, she never liked Andrew," Shannon mused. "I guess that was another red flag I missed."

"Since we aren't in a hurry, could we walk her around the lake?"

"She would love it. I didn't get a chance to walk her much this morning."

With the leash in one hand and Shannon's hand in the other, Max opened the door. As they walked on the trail, Shannon's anxiety melted away. Funny how he always had a calming effect on her. *God, thank you for Max.*

Halfway around the lake, under a large oak tree, Max stopped and faced Shannon. "I've wanted to kiss you all day. This seems like a perfect spot." He was all smiles. When she smiled back, he embraced her, caressed and stroked her face, and gazed into her eyes until their lips met.

Shannon felt weak in his arms—she had never been kissed like that before, ever. He pulled her closer to his chest, holding her firmly yet gently. Surely he could hear her heart pounding. *I've been in love with him all this time—why didn't I realize it?*

He stepped back and looked at her. "Shannon, I love you. I truly do."

"Max, I love you too. I'm sure now." Another longer kiss followed.

"I've longed to hear you say those words."

"I don't know why I didn't acknowledge it before. I think I felt obligated to try to reconcile with Andrew . . . maybe even a little bit of false guilt and thinking I was somehow responsible for the marriage ending. I'm sorry I made you wait all this time." Willow tugged at the leash, so they resumed their walk. "Does any of this make sense?"

"Of course it does—because you're compassionate and honorable, and you wanted to give him a second chance. I understand and, though it wasn't what I wanted, I respected your decision. It was for the right reasons, and it proves how much you esteem marriage. That's a very admirable quality, one of many you have." He squeezed her hand.

"I'm glad you understand. That means a lot."

"It's all behind us now. And, like I told you a while ago, you are worth the wait. So very worth the wait."

"Thank you for waiting." They finished the rest of the trail and went inside. As Shannon got ready to leave, Max wandered through the living area.

"Hey, the plant on your table—isn't it the same kind Rose has all over her shop, the amaryllis plant?" He picked up the pot for a closer look. "She told me about them when I interviewed her."

"Yes. Those three buds are about ready to bloom. I think they'll be pink and white when they open. Possibly like the pin she wears every day. Did you know her late husband gave it to her?"

"Guys aren't too observant, but it would be hard not to notice that pin. Didn't know the reason though. Ready to go?"

"Yes. All set."

Chapter Twenty-One ❧

Shannon spent Monday and Tuesday night on the phone with Max. They decided they couldn't wait for the weekend to see each other again, so they planned for dinner and a movie on Wednesday after work. Every moment she spent with Max was enthralling. She wondered how much longer her heart would skip a beat when she saw him—she didn't want to lose the pleasurable sensation. Jen, Claire, and her parents all expressed happiness and excitement when she called to tell them.

She breezed into the Amaryllis on Saturday morning, love showing on her face. "Good morning, Rose," she practically sang.

"My, you look mighty happy this morning. Might it have something to do with Mr. Maxwell Harrington?"

"Oh, you know. I keep forgetting how quickly news spreads in this little town." She laughed. "Yes, I'm in love, Rose—really in love. I don't know why I couldn't follow my heart before. But I'm so grateful he didn't give up on me."

"I didn't think he would. It was obvious to everyone—except you, apparently—that he was madly in love with you. Every time he saw you, he lit up. And, dear, you lit up also, even though you tried to hide it. No one who saw you together was fooled. You just had to work some things out in your life, didn't you?"

"I guess that's one way of looking at it. I've been thinking I was pretty stupid and blinded. But there's a new chapter now, and it's a beautiful one."

"Beautiful, indeed. Max is a wonderful man. I've known him for several years. I'm delighted for both of you."

"Thank you—I'm pretty happy for us too." She couldn't help the grin on her face. "Oh, and I almost forgot to tell you—my amaryllis is about ready to bloom. Three blossoms."

"Very appropriate timing, I might say." Rose nodded, then turned to greet a customer when the bell over the door rang.

"Hey, Shannon," Madelaine said quietly as she walked in from the gardens. "Heard you have a new beau. I met him a few weeks ago. He seems like a great guy. Rose sure speaks highly of him."

"Thank you. He's wonderful. We dated before you started here." She shook her head. "I never should have ended our relationship. But we're back on track now, and everything's great."

"I'm happy for you," Madelaine said as she pulled the orders for the day and then assisted another customer.

Shannon was in the Tea Cozy, pulling the first batch of raspberry scones out of the oven, when she heard a commotion in the florist shop. She set the tray on the counter and went to see what was happening.

Two police officers were at the counter with Rose—and she was wailing loudly. Shannon recognized Officer Garonna, who had his arm around Rose and was speaking quietly to her.

Shannon rushed over, arriving at the same time as Madelaine, who came up from the workroom.

"Rose, what's wrong?"

Rose shook her head, unable to respond. The other officer introduced himself.

"I'm Chief Purnell," he said. "She's okay, nothing's wrong. Give her a minute."

Shannon brought her a box of tissues. Rose wiped her teary eyes, patted her chest, and took several deep breaths. "Thank You, God. Thank You." she repeated between tearful moments. Shannon was bewildered. What had her so upset, and why would she be thanking God for it?

The chief turned to Madelaine. "Would you ladies lock the doors and put the closed sign in the window? You could add a note stating the shop will reopen later, maybe at eleven o'clock?" He turned and continued speaking quietly to Rose.

Rose reached out a hand to Shannon. "I can't explain at this moment, but I'm fine." She stopped to catch her breath. "I'm better than fine—I'm wonderful. These are happy tears, and tears of relief. I'm going to the cottage with Chief Purnell and Officer Garonna—we'll be back soon to explain. Not to worry. Just enjoy a break next door." She managed a watery smile and joined the officers on the way to the cottage.

Returning from locking up, Madelaine said, "Those are the officers who were here before—who upset Rose last week. I can't imagine what's going on. Do you have any idea?"

"Not a clue. But I'm glad it isn't bad news—the way she was sobbing, I thought someone had died."

"Me too. Geez, it was awful to see her like that." With nothing else to do, the girls wandered into the Tea Cozy and sat down. Madelaine grinned at Shannon. "So tell me more about your Mister Right, since we have some free time."

Twenty minutes later, the officers came into the Cozy to talk to them. "Rose is fine. She's making some important, long overdue calls to her family. She'll come in to talk to you after she's finished. I'm sorry to keep you in the dark, but it's her story to tell—and it has a wonderfully happy ending." A satisfied smile lit the police chief's face.

"Thank you for letting us know," Shannon replied. "We're concerned, but we're glad to know she's okay."

As the chief left the building, Officer Garonna turned her way. "So, Shannon, how are you doing? Is your ex leaving you alone?"

She shrugged uncomfortably. "Not entirely. He showed up here again, right after you released him, before I went home. He was pretty insistent that I should talk to him, but Rose chased him off. And at some point, he left a note in my mailbox repeating the same thing."

"Are you feeling safe?"

"Maybe not as secure as I was before." Actually, she was glad he was asking the questions now.

"Could you elaborate?"

"Well, I just thought he had too much to drink that day you were here, and things would die down naturally. But he's not getting the message that the relationship is over. I've asked him not to call or text, but he's messaging me several times a day. Most of his texts are very demanding. He keeps insisting that we meet. I've been looking out windows and through parking lots to see if his car is there . . . I never did that before." Anxiety returned as she talked about it, and she bit her lip.

"We mentioned a restraining order. Do you want to file for your protection?"

"Before, I would have said no way. Now I'm thinking it might be a good idea. He still seems to be angry, and I'm not used to him that way. Rose keeps saying it might be a good idea too."

He nodded. "Stop by the station first chance you get—today if you have time. Your protection is our first priority."

"Thank you. I'll stop by this afternoon." She knew now it was the right decision.

"Sounds good. Wise." He shook her hand. "Goodbye, ladies."

Rose finally returned and sat at the table with them. She looked completely different than when she'd left. Now she was radiant and happy.

"Oh, girls, have I got a lot to tell you two—or like my mother used to say, I've got a lot of 'splainin' to do." She laughed breathily and patted her hair. "Oh dear, I don't know where to start. Let's grab another cup of tea. This could be a long conversation."

When all the cups were refilled, she began. "My name is not Rose Daniels—it's Ruth Decker." Shannon and Madelaine both reacted in shock.

"I'm from Washington state and all my family is still there. I just spoke to each of my children on the phone. Thank God, I could reach them." She sighed in relief.

"My first husband, Benjamin Decker, was killed in a hiking accident, and I was alone for several years. He was the love of my life—a wonderful man. Then I met Roland Cranston. He was wealthy, influential in the community, and very charming—he swept this unsuspecting widow off her feet."

She took a deep breath. "Unfortunately, he was not who I thought he was. Not long after we were married, I found out he was controlling and abusive and a heavy drinker. A few years later, I discovered he was dealing drugs—heavy-duty drugs—and laundering money. I confronted him and wanted to divorce him, but he threatened to harm my family if I went to the police or pursued a divorce. So I told no one what I had discovered—I lived in constant fear on the inside, but I had to keep convincing my family that all was well."

She looked at Shannon. "That's why I've been so concerned about you, dear. I saw the same dark anger inside Andrew's eyes that I saw in Roland's."

"I'm so sorry, Rose. And thank you for your concern for me."

She nodded, her eyes dark with memory. "My life changed in one moment—a delivery man rang my doorbell one afternoon, and I answered it. He was standing on the sidewalk with a bouquet of flowers. He asked if I was Ruth and when I replied, he pulled out a handgun and fired—hit me in the chest—then he quickly drove off."

"What!" Madelaine and Shannon exclaimed at the same moment.

"Yes, but God protected me. You see, the bullet hit my amaryllis pin." She took off her pin and placed it on the table. "It miraculously deflected the bullet. See this part here?" She stroked the damaged petal. "I always wore the pin over my heart, because my dear Benjamin had given it to me. And still, he protected me. It was a miracle that I survived. The impact knocked me to the ground where a neighbor found me and called the police and an ambulance."

"Oh, Rose, I can't begin to imagine what that was like. I'm so sorry this happened to you." Madelaine's eyes were wide as she patted Rose's hand.

"While I was in the hospital, I told the police I suspected Roland had hired the shooter but there was no proof. I couldn't even give a description because it all happened so quickly. I didn't have proof of the other things I'd found out about him either, but they were already investigating him. Some of Roland's business partners were on the police radar for suspected drug dealing, but they hadn't found any viable connection to him yet. I told them if they ever had enough evidence to convict him, I would testify. I was too afraid to go home, and I didn't want to go near my family and draw them into danger, but I knew God had protected me and was giving me a second chance. There were enough other domestic violence calls on my record that the police agreed to help me change my name and Social Security number so I could start over somewhere far away. I ended up here, and I've been happy, but I haven't seen any of my family since I moved here. Chief Purnell, Officer Garonna, and Pastor Dalton are the only people who know who I really am."

Her eyes brightened. "But everything changed today. The police finally had a strong enough case against him to arrest him, but he and the men who were with him fought back. His own guy shot him. He's dead—" She stopped suddenly and took a shaky breath. "I'm sorry that he died . . . I don't think he knew Christ."

Shannon hugged her, her eyes brimming with sympathy. "Well, knowing you, Rose—Ruth?—that wasn't for lack of knowing."

"No, no it wasn't." Rose shook her head sadly, then straightened. "But—my son is making airline reservations for me right now. I'm going to fly to Washington to see everyone. I can't wait!" A brilliant smile broke through the lingering tears. "I've prayed for this day for a very long time." She stopped talking, her eyes fixed on some distant plane. Moments later, she drew a long breath then looked closely at Shannon, then Madelaine.

"So. I need to figure out what to do with the shop. I'm thinking I can reduce the hours to accommodate the times you two can be here. Do you think that would work? Would you mind taking over for me for a little while?"

"I'd love to." Madelaine said.

At the same time, Shannon said, "Of course. We can make it work. That's the last thing you should be worried about now."

"I appreciate it very much—I know I'm leaving this place in very capable hands." Rose smiled. "Now, I have some happy packing to do—I'll be in touch when I get to Washington." She hugged both of them, then hurried back to the cottage.

Shannon and Madelaine sat back down at the table, still stunned from the revelation.

"Whoa!" Shannon said. "That's quite a story. I can't believe what she's been through."

"I know—she sure sacrificed a lot to keep her children and grandchildren safe." Madelaine scratched her head, still trying to absorb the news. "A lot of pieces are starting to come together, though."

"Exactly. Things have been a little weird lately. Sure never expected it would be something like this. What a family reunion she's about to have."

Madelaine looked at the clock. "It's almost eleven. You ready to open?"

"Yeah. Let's keep this as quiet as we can, okay? Whatever gets out, it's Rose's story to tell, like the chief said."

Madelaine nodded. "Agreed. I don't even want to try to figure out those details."

The days passed, and Shannon and Madelaine worked out a schedule with Rose's regular volunteers to keep the Amaryllis open and working at full capacity. For those customers who asked, they told people Rose was on a well-deserved vacation. Most were delighted to hear it and asked no more questions.

Shannon shared the news with Max, who was both happy and relieved to finally have answers to the questions that had been bothering him for so long. She couldn't help but laugh as she watched his reporter's mind kick into gear.

"Just think, Shannon. A story like this could go viral. Maybe she'll let me do an exclusive. It's an amazing tale."

"I'll ask her if she calls."

Rose called the shop a few times each week, and three weeks later, she made plans to return home. Shannon, Madelaine, and Max, now volunteering too, worked busily to make sure everything was perfect in the shop.

Friday evening, just before closing, a cab dropped Rose off at the front door. Max hurried to open the door for her and greeted her with a hug.

"Thank you, Max. Ahh, home at last." Her long sigh was followed by a beaming smile. "I've missed you all."

Shannon and Madelaine caught her in a group hug. "We've missed you too. Welcome home."

"The shop looks wonderful—better than I left it. Girls, I can never thank you enough for everything." Turning to Max, she added, "And I understand you helped too. Thank you."

"It was my pleasure," he said. "Here, let me take your bags to the cottage."

She handed him the keys. "Thank you."

Shannon reached to give Rose another hug, and as she did, her sweater got caught on the amaryllis pin. "This pin!" She laughed as she disentangled herself. "Oh, my plant finally bloomed while you were gone. You should have seen it. It was glorious. And it must be the same variety as this—it was the same pink and white."

"Hmm, imagine that." Rose winked knowingly. A yawn caught her by surprise. "Excuse me. Well, girls, it's been a long day, so I'm going to the cottage. I'll see you both tomorrow morning." And with that, she walked through the back door and disappeared into the cottage.

On Saturday, Rose agreed to give Max the full story, so after church on Sunday, he and Shannon returned to the cottage for the interview. He made a recording, shot a video, and took several photographs of Rose in her shop, the gardens, and the Tea Cozy. Then he took off to write the article.

The newspaper released Max's article the next weekend. Remembering the reaction after his first piece on the Amaryllis, Shannon and Max both took the day off from work, expecting the shop would be extra busy. They were right. Customers arrived singly and in groups, eager to talk to Rose. Some had actual copies of the newspaper and wanted her to autograph the article, while others had seen the piece online and were coming in to celebrate.

Max had picked up on one of Rose's phrases for describing her work and used it in the article, and her "perfect imperfections" were flying off the shelves. Shannon and Madelaine rushed to keep up with arranging bouquets to fill them. Other volunteers kept the Tea Cozy and the registers running smoothly. Rose was absolutely glowing—everyone commented on it. The shop simply buzzed with excitement.

When closing time finally came, Max put the sign in the window and congratulated Rose on a spectacular day.

"All thanks to you," she said with a hug.

"My favorite person to interview, by far." He smiled.

Shannon and Madelaine straightened up the counter and closed out the registers. Then they joined Rose and Max and the rest of the day's volunteers in the Tea Cozy for refreshments. Everyone was pleased with the results of the day.

"I want to thank you all for being here today. We needed the extra hands, for sure," Rose said. "I'm sure you're all exhausted."

"The excitement was invigorating," Shannon answered. "We're all just happy we could be a part of the celebration, Rose."

"Isn't this the most wonderful little town? So supportive." Rose said cheerfully.

"That it is." Max added. "That it is."

The party wound down, and the volunteers began to leave. Shannon worked her way through the room, picking up trash and straightening chairs. When Rose realized what she was doing, she hurried over.

"Oh, don't worry about cleaning up, dear. I'll be up early in the morning. And really, you don't need to come in tomorrow. You've been such a big help."

"I'll be here, Rose. It's my home away from home, you know." She grinned and squeezed Rose's shoulder affectionately.

"Well, it's certainly appreciated—always."

❦

Customer traffic was still heavy the next week as Rose's story spread around. It was a good thing she'd had a large inventory of adorned containers in the back room—everything she had left was now displayed on the shelves in the shop.

Saturday afternoon, Max stopped by just before closing time. He kissed Shannon on the cheek, then turned to Rose.

"Rose, do you have a minute?"

"Of course," she replied. They walked to the Tea Cozy.

Shannon locked the door after the last customer, then freshened up and joined them at a thankfulness table. Rose excused herself to close up the register.

"What is this," Shannon asked, pointing to a placemat on the table. "Rose must be doing something new—I've never seen placemats here before."

Max stepped between her and the table and took her hands in his. "Shannon, you know I love you, right?"

"Of course I do. And I love you." She was still looking at the table.

He squeezed her hand, then turned. Catching hold of the placemat nearest her, he pulled it away, revealing a handwritten note on the tablecloth. He watched as she read the words, then he repeated them aloud.

"Shannon Amelia Enright, I am thankful for you. Will you marry me?"

Shannon looked up, momentarily stunned. A bright smile blossomed across her face as she emphatically replied, "Yes. Yes!"

Max pulled a small black box from his pocket, opened it, and placed it in her hand.

"Oh, Max, it's beautiful . . . absolutely beautiful." Tears streamed down her face.

Max placed the ring gently on her finger. "I love you with all my heart," he murmured. Then he stood up and looked toward the doors. "She said yes," he shouted.

Rose and Madelaine came in with balloons and flowers, followed by Shannon's parents, Max's parents, Claire, Mark, and

Charlotte Amelia, Jen and Kevin, Pastor Dalton, Libby, and several of Shannon's and Max's coworkers.

"What?!" Shannon turned to Max. "Where—how'd you do this?"

"They were all waiting in the cottage. It would have been really bad if you'd said no," he said with a laugh.

Rose chimed in, "I don't think there was any doubt she'd say yes, Max."

The newspaper photographer pointed to a camera in the corner, revealing he had captured everything on video.

Shannon's father cleared his throat, getting everyone's attention. "For those who don't know me, I'm Shannon's father. I haven't known Max long, but I like him and respect him. He drove to New York and asked for our blessing, a very admirable action. Max, you've made my daughter very happy—the happiest I've ever seen her. Thank you. Shannon, my beautiful daughter, I've seen you grow through some tough times in the last year or so, and I couldn't be more proud of the woman you've become. Now, to both of you, I wish you the happiest life together."

Max kissed his fiancée . . . and then kissed her again, a little longer. Lively cheers and congratulations filled the room.

Caterers arrived with food and extra chairs, starting the festive party.

"Max, everything is perfect. I'm so happy—you've thought of everything. Thank you."

"All my pleasure, my lovely bride-to-be."

"Oh, and that can't happen soon enough." She laughed. After the guests left, Shannon took Max by the hand and led him back to the thankfulness table where he had proposed. Clutching a marker, she wrote "YES!" in large letters, signed her name, and added the date. Max signed his name above hers.

"Now, it's perfect." she said.

Epilogue 🌹

*E*xactly two months from the day of the engagement party, Shannon peeked out the back door of the shop into the gardens. A beautiful white arch, covered in white roses and ivy, stood at the end of the center pathway. Friends and family filled the chairs arranged on either side. It was almost time.

At the end of the pathway, Pastor Dalton, Max, and his best man filed out to stand under the arch. Shannon's heartbeat picked up. Claire reached over and gave her arm a quick squeeze, then headed down the aisle, her arms full of white roses and ivy.

Dad leaned over and, with a beaming smile, asked, "Ready?"

"Absolutely," Shannon declared.

Claire reached her spot at the archway. The pianist began to play "A Thousand Years," and Shannon and her father stepped out onto the path.

Max's face beamed with pride as his bride, radiant in a white lace gown, her long golden curls topped with a delicate pearl headband, made her way toward him.

She reached the archway, handed her amaryllis-and-rose bouquet to Claire, and looked back to her father. He gave her a quick kiss on the cheek, then stepped aside for Max.

❧

A week later, they returned to Max's house—now their home. They popped in at the Amaryllis to see Rose and share the memorable events of their time in St. Lucia.

"Oh, what a lovely honeymoon. I'm so happy for you two. Absolutely lovely." Rose said, admiring the photos on Max's computer. "I have some news—I bought a small condo in Washington, near my family. I'm planning to spend a few months there each year. Shannon, I'm wondering if you would be my manager here at the Amaryllis. I'll need more help now."

"I'm honored, Rose, that you would ask me." She gave Rose a big hug. "Your shop—and you—have made such a difference in my life. There's just something about this place that touches hearts and helps things make sense. I'd like nothing better. Thank you."

Max looked on proudly, fully confident that this arrangement would bring good things to all their lives. "You're a lovely woman, Rose," he said. "I thank God for the part you played through Shannon's difficult days, for your faithful presence that brought her back to Him." He pulled his wife close. "And me."

Order Information

To order additional copies of this book, please visit
www.redemption-press.com.
Also available on Amazon.com and BarnesandNoble.com
or by calling toll-free 1-844-2REDEEM.

CPSIA information can be obtained
at www.ICGtesting.com
Printed in the USA
LVHW030614220720
661196LV00006B/416